HAPPILY EVER AFTERLIFE

Crushed

HAPPILY EVER AFTERLIFE

Crushed

by Orli Zuravicky

SCHOLASTIC INC.

HAPPILY EVER AFTERLIFE

For my dad, who has been
my guide, my champion,
and my Giving Tree

ISBN 978-0-545-93257-8

10 9 8 7 6 5 4 3 2 1   16 17 18 19 20

Printed in the U.S.A.   40
First printing 2016

Book design by Jennifer Rinaldi

LIMBO CENTRAL
MIDDLE SCHOOL

It's time for fall season's
CHEERLEADING tryouts!
Do you have rhythm?
Are you flexible?
Do you want to share
your school spirit?
Come to the football field
on Wednesday evening
at five o'clock sharp with a prepared
routine and show us what you've got.

See you all there!
Your Cheerleading Captain,
GEORGIA SINCLAIRE

THE
LIMBO CENTRAL
CLUB MANUAL

RULE #1:

All students must join at least one club within their first month at Limbo. There are many clubs to choose from, so be sure to explore all of your options.

Chapter One
I Cheer, You Cheer

Lucy Chadwick . . . Ghostcoming Queen. It has a nice ring to it, doesn't it? To be fair, *technically* I could be the Ghostcoming *King*, since I entered Limbo Central Middle School's dance-a-thon with my best friend, Cecily Vanderberg, and we won the title of King and Queen together.

Either way? I'm ghost royalty.

(FYI . . . I'm not joking—I'm *actually* a ghost. How, you ask? Because I'm kind of, sort of, completely . . . well, dead. But it's all good, I promise!)

Anyway, becoming Limbo Central royalty isn't a bad way to end your first two weeks in the afterlife—especially when your first day started with you developing a giant crush on Colin Reed, your older ghost tutor, which caused some ugly beef with his mean-girl girlfriend. Or should I say EX-GIRLFRIEND.

Smiley face.

Okay, okay, I know that sounds harsh, but this girl—Georgia Sinclaire—makes normal mean girls look like UNICEF volunteers! For example, on my first day as a ghost at Limbo she literally threw a ball through my head. I was pretty see-through because I was newly dead, so thankfully it didn't hurt. But it felt super weird, and, honestly, that's just rude. Then, last week, when I finally had enough energy to become solid, she threw another one at my head—and that one hit me! I had to go to the nurse and everything. So, yeah, she's definitely getting what's coming to her.

"Are you ready to go?" Cecily calls to me from inside our bathroom.

We're not only best friends, we're also roommates. I crossed over, like, a day before she did, so we've been learning everything together. Cool, right? And the best part is that we were friends even *before* we got to the afterlife, so we know each other super well.

T.G.

(Thank ghostliness. Get it?!)

Because leaving everything behind and trying to figure out your new way of afterlife all by yourself is crazy hard—not to mention lonely. Having each other here is THE BEST.

Afterlife friends forever.

"One sec," I answer, getting my books together. I can finally carry my own backpack now, which is one of those things that you don't normally care about until you're suddenly unable to do it. Then you're all like, what?! See, when you first become a ghost you need to figure out how to harness and use energy in a different way so you can interact with stuff. It's super complicated and *totally* not worth getting into. The point? I can now carry things like a normal ghostly type person.

Yay!

"It's seven forty-five," she warns gently.

It's Monday morning, and if we don't get moving we're going to be late for school. That's when I notice something appear on the Tabulator screen.

"Oh goody, we got a message from Georgia," I inform Cecily as she exits the bathroom.

"We did? Just us? What does it say?"

"No, not just us. The whole school. It's about Cheerleading tryouts—on Wednesday evening."

"Oh."

Cecily falls silent after that.

For a while last week she was thinking about joining the squad as her required club, but I thought I had talked her out of it.

As we walk over to school, I feel her out on the subject again.

"You still want to start our own dance club, don't you?" I ask, reminding her of our significantly more-awesome-than-cheerleading idea.

"Sure," Cecily replies.

Cecily and I were both ballerinas. Well, *are* both ballerinas, I guess I should say. When we crossed over, we were both stuck in our dance costumes from rehearsal. Another one of the Limbo Rules is that you have to stay in the clothes you came over in until you can harness enough energy to change them yourself. No one else can change them for you. So . . . there we were, waddling around school in our pointe shoes and tutus for, like, two weeks!

So mortifying.

Thankfully we're finally learning enough ghost skills and gaining enough strength to change our clothes—at least minimally. I seriously couldn't take another week of walking around in those torture devices!

"But," she continues, "it could take a really long time to make the club happen. Who knows how many hoops we'll have to jump through to get it off the ground. Cheerleading might be fun, you know, in the meantime."

I don't like where this is heading.

Hmph.

"How can anything involving Georgia Sinclaire be remotely fun?"

"I know she's the captain, but she's not the only girl on the squad. Chloe is on it, and so are a lot of other girls we don't even know yet."

"The jury's still out on Chloe," I remind her.

Chloe McAvoy spent the last two weeks (and probably most of her afterlife before that) being Georgia's mostly mute, wicked sidekick, until the Ghostcoming dance, when she *seemed* to realize that Georgia doesn't really care about her and only likes her because she does everything Georgia tells her to do.

"*You're* the one who welcomed Chloe into our group at the dance," Cecily reminds me. "You convinced her she could find new friends who would be nicer to her than Georgia and actually listen to what she has to say."

"I know, I know. But, maybe Georgia got her hooks back into her by now? She's quick, that one."

"Even so, after what Georgia did at Ghostcoming? I'm pretty sure we can take her if she does anything sneaky."

"If? Uhm, hello! *Sneaky* is, like, her middle name. It's either that or *Completely Evil*. I can't quite remember which," I joke.

"Those aren't middle names, those are nicknames," she corrects me.

"When did *you* become Cecily 'Literal Girl' Vanderberg?"

"Ha-ha. Look, I never got to be on the squad at my old school because of ballet. I just think it will be fun. Being cheerful's my thing! Plus, it'll be a great way to meet cute boys."

"I thought you liked Marcus?" I ask, confused. Marcus Riley is a guy in our new circle of friends. He plays guitar in a band called Figure of Speech (which yours truly helped name!) with four other guys.

"He's cute, but I'm not carving our initials into desks just yet—not like you and Colin . . ." she teases.

Ahhh . . . Colin. My heart quickens at the sound of his name, and I've already had at least ten Lady-and-the-Tramp-style daydreams since I woke up this morning! Me and Colin sharing an ice-cream cone; me and Colin sharing a breadstick; me and Colin sharing a piece of licorice (FYI, the licorice fantasy turned accidentally violent, given the candy's tough and inflexible nature, so do not try this at home!). All these daydreams despite the fact that the death of his relationship with Georgia is so new it hasn't even crossed over yet.

Ha-ha, get it?

"Right . . ." I say. "Well, exactly *nothing* has happened with me and Colin since the dance on Saturday night. He's officially broken up with Georgia, but that's about all the progress we've made."

"I'm sure he'll notice your lovely new ensemble today and say something super sweet to you," Cecily says, all perky-like.

I've changed my tights into slightly heavier leggings, ditched the tutu (hurrah!), put on a long cardigan over my leotard, and traded in my pointe shoes for Converse.

Sweet relief!

"Unless he's changed his mind and decided he's over me and just wants to be friends," I say, unsure.

The truth is, when he broke up with Georgia at the dance, I was certain he was going to ask me out right then and there. And he kind of did, I suppose, at the end, when he made me promise to watch *Star Wars* with him. But then he never specified a time or place. Who does that?! Hello, boys? If you're going to make a date with a girl, you have to *actually* pick a date! Even though yesterday was Sunday, and would have been perfect for our first date, the day came and went without a word from him.

Sad face.

"Don't be crazy!" Cecily says. "That won't happen. He's cuckoo for you."

We get to school a few minutes before the first bell rings, and walking down the hallway feels like that moment when you realize the weird thing you thought only happened in your dream *actually* happened in real life, except you can't decide if that's good or bad.

Spotlight much?

I immediately spy Colin across the hallway, and it takes all of my energy (which is considerable when you realize that I need it to do a lot of other more important things like, say, touch the ground when I walk) to refrain from running over to him and throwing myself into his arms like he's a soldier who's just returned home from battle. Luckily the bell rings and I snap out of my crazy.

First period on Mondays, Wednesdays, and Fridays I have Famous Apparitions. Thankfully Mia Bennett—another member of our inner crew—is in my class. Last class we learned about the Brown Lady of Raynham, who likes to hang around a famous mansion called Raynham Hall in England. Apparently she's been seen by a lot of people. I bet that's totally against ghost rules. Ms. Roslyn said the Brown Lady—her real name is Lady Townshend—was actually going to come in and tell us the story *herself*, but she had a last-minute change of plans . . .

I wonder if those plans included haunting Raynham Hall, by any chance?!

Weirdo.

"Hey, Lucy!" Mia says happily, sitting down at the desk next to mine. "How was the rest of your weekend? Did you and Cecily celebrate your victory in style?"

"Being the Queen is hard work," I joke. "Actually we pretty much did nothing yesterday. How about you and Trey?"

Trey Abbot is Mia's boyfriend. They're ridiculously adorable.

"Same," she replies, taking out her textbook and notepad. "That's what Sundays are for, isn't it?"

"Totally," I reply. "Hey, do you know anyone who would want to join a new dance club Cecily and I are starting? We only have two weeks before we need to officially join something, so I want to get this thing up and running."

"Well, not that you need any more drama with Georgia, but pretty much everyone on the Cheerleading team is a good bet."

"Right . . . Any other ideas?"

"Uhm, last year we had a Winter Wonderland talent show, and I'm pretty sure I remember there being at least two, maybe three, dance routines. You could ask Ms. Keaner for the list of acts and participants and go talk to them?"

"That's a great idea, thanks! Cecily is about ten seconds away from joining the Cheerleading team 'in the meantime.' If she joins, it would be the worst."

"Because of Georgia?"

"Pretty much."

"She can't be *that* bad. I mean, it's a school activity, so Georgia has a whole team to answer to, plus the coach. Hopefully she's on better behavior as captain than she is as just a normal person."

"I'd rather not find out . . ."

"I hear you. It was pretty cruel what she did to you guys at the dance."

Long story short? Basically the Ghostcoming dance was themed, and when Georgia saw that Cecily and I had managed to alter our ballet outfits to fit the theme, she told the principal we disobeyed the Limbo Rules! It was a mess. But in the end, we totally bested her.

In your face (mean girl).

"Yeah, well, I'm hoping the next two weeks of my afterlife won't be all about Georgia like the first two weeks were," I reply. " 'Cause boy, is that getting boring!"

"So," Mia says, "you know that the clubs at Limbo are a bit different from the clubs at your old middle school down in the World of the Living, right? I mean, Ms. Keaner probably told you that already, didn't she?"

"Uh, no, she didn't tell me. What does that mean?"

"Oh. Well, it means that they all have to utilize some ghost skill or power. Remember how the Ghostcoming football game wasn't just ordinary football?"

"Yeah?"

"It's like that with every club. At the newspaper, the *Limbolater*, we have to use our powers to report on things that happen down in the World of the Living as well as up here in Limbo. The Chess Club plays by moving the pieces with energy. On Track, we have to build our own hurdles as we run. We have a certain number we need to jump over and they need to be a specific height, and so on. Cheerleading is the same—it's not just regular cheerleading, it's flying and floating and lifting other people up with your energy, writing the cheers above your head in the air, stuff like that."

"Oh."

Just when I thought I was getting the hang of this ghost thing.

"But you're catching on to everything so quickly," Mia says, encouragingly. "I'm sure this will be the same way."

"Okay, but that means we need to come up with a way for our dance club to be . . . supernaturally inclined, right?"

"Right."

"Any ideas?"

"Nope."

"Awesome."

"Off topic? Figure of Speech is playing at the Clairvoyance Café on Wednesday night. You and Cecily have to come!"

"Cool! Oh—no, wait. That's the same night as the Cheerleading tryouts, isn't it?"

I wonder if Georgia did that on purpose, but I don't say that out loud.

"Well, the band doesn't go on until six o'clock."

"Okay, we'll be there. I'm sure Cecily will be excited to see Marcus in action. Ooh, maybe he'll invite her himself?? That would be soooo cute!"

Just then the second bell rings. "Okay, please take your seats and settle down," Ms. Roslyn says. "Let's begin with chapter five, 'Apparitions of the Twentieth Century'."

The first two periods crawl by, and eventually it's time to face the music: my Psychic Education class with Georgia and Chloe. The class during which I refuse to let Georgia throw any more balls at my head. Now that I dethroned her at the dance, she should be feeling relatively on guard.

But you never know what to expect with this girl.

"Okay, ladies," Coach Trellis says, "today we're going to start our gymnastics rotation. We'll be working on floor routines first. Here's how it will go: We teach you a routine, and then you will perform it in groups. Everyone come into the center of the room and spread out."

We all do as we're told, and when I look to my right I notice Chloe is standing next to me.

"Hey," she says, quietly.

"Hey."

"How was the rest of your weekend?" she asks.

She's being friendly, and I can tell she's trying to show me whose side she's on after the whole dance disaster. I get a warm, fuzzy feeling inside. It's nice to know that something you've said has made a big difference. I mean, Georgia is the worst friend to Chloe. She never listens to her or asks her opinion about anything. It's always all about Georgia. I'm really happy Chloe knows it doesn't have to be like that anymore. I even feel a little bit bad about having doubted her before.

Whoops.

"It was pretty low-key," I reply. "How about yours?"

"I went shopping with Briana."

"Who's Briana?"

"Briana Clark? She's a second year. She's on the Cheerleading squad with me, I'll introduce you sometime. Anyway, the new fall fashion ideas are out, so we wanted to see what's in this season."

Another thing about Limbo? You don't actually buy clothes. You pay for outfit *ideas*. Because ghosts use energy to change their outfits and appearance, stores don't need to sell actual clothing. They just sell the idea of new fashions— and the instructions on how to make them, if you need them. Weird, huh? Don't get me wrong, it's heaven not having to spend crazy amounts of money on new clothes, but heaven still doesn't come cheap. It's SUPER time- and energy-consuming to make your own clothes out of THIN AIR!

The job of a fashion designer is way more intense than I imagined.

Respect.

"That sounds fun. Find anything you like?"

"I saw an awesome plaid shirt dress with this chunky belt that I'm gonna try to re-create. Georgia never would have let me do it, you know, *before*. She says plaid is for the 'fashionably challenged.'"

"I *love* plaid," I say, with a smile. "I think it's very retro chic."

"Okay, settle down," Coach Trellis says, and when I look up I notice that the whole class is spread out as we were told, except for Georgia, who's standing up in front of all of us next to Coach.

Coach Trellis continues speaking. "I've asked Georgia to help me teach the routine, since she has the most gymnastics experience from her cheerleading."

You've got to be kidding me.

Grrr.

I wish Coach had asked me to help. I mean, I did just win a dance-a-thon. Besides, everyone knows that ballet dancers are way more graceful than cheerleaders. I'm not trying to be snobby, or anything, it's just, well, we're essentially more graceful than *everyone*—it's, like, our job.

Whatever.

I don't know why this is bothering me so much, anyway. It's just a gym class. Besides, maybe this is a good thing? This way I can see what Georgia is like as a teacher, and what she'll be like as a captain. If she's as bad as I think she'll be, I can take that back to Cecily and use it to convince her to not join the Cheerleading squad. And if she's good? Well, then maybe I'll have less to worry about.

But probably not.

"Okay, the first thing we're going to do is some floor poses," she says. "Watch me and repeat what I do."

Then Georgia gets down on her right knee, pulls her right foot toward the back of her hip, twisting her body all the way to the right.

Easy breezy.

Then she slowly lifts herself off the floor in the same exact position. For a few seconds, she just hovers there over the mat. Then she slowly drifts back down.

Ghost powers be darned.

"Okay, we'll try the position only first before we try to lift off the ground," she says. "Let's see what you've got."

The class gets down on the floor and tries to mimic her, but most of them can't even get close.

"Ouch, this hurts!" cries one girl.

"Why is this necessary?" asks another.

"Is it supposed to look all twisted like this?"

Georgia makes her way around the room, helping to pose the rest of the class. Coach Trellis makes her way around, too, but she's a lot less helpful. In fact, I'm pretty sure she can't tell a split leap from a split pea.

After a few minutes, Georgia comes up behind me. My pose is perfect, and I'm not just saying that. I do this stretch about twenty times a week before ballet class because it hits your quad muscles and your back at the same time.

Bring it, girl.

"Ladies," she calls out, "look at Lucy's positioning. She's doing this move perfectly. Try to copy her."

I'm in shock. There's no way Georgia's saying something nice just because. There has to be some kind of ulterior motive. With this girl? There's always something. Unless . . . by some crazy chance, everything that happened at the dance finally made her rethink how she treats people?

Then she crouches down low behind me and whispers in my ear, "This thing between you and me? It isn't over. Not by a long shot."

Yeah.

So . . . like I said, she's always got some ulterior motive. And if Cecily joins the Cheerleading Squad, I can tell you exactly what Georgia is going to do:

1. Shower Cecily with fake attention
2. Weasel her way into becoming Cecily's BFF
3. Enact some other kind of revenge that I can't think of right now, but I know will be THE WORST

Despite being the best at tackling the pose on the ground, when it's time to lift up off it, I have a teensy bit of trouble.

And by teensy, I mean tons.

Georgia's words keep echoing in my head, and the more I think about her, the more frustrated I get. What should be a gentle hover a few inches above the ground turns into me shooting myself up in the air like a cannonball and hitting my head on the ceiling.

Ouch.

"Lucy, please be careful," Georgia reprimands, as if I did it on purpose. "As you can see, integrating your ghost skills with your former life skills isn't quite as easy as some might think."

I can't believe I'm actually about to say this, but . . . Georgia is (GASP!) right.

For the next half an hour, Georgia stands up in front of us acting all better than everyone and correcting people left and right. I'm so annoyed I could scream! But I don't. Instead, I decide that the sweetest revenge is to beat her at her own game, or should I say, club. I need to seriously up my skills. If Cecily joins Cheerleading, she'll never quit. Georgia is out for blood, and Cecily cheerleading is her meal ticket.

Vampire-style.

By the time class ends, I'm so amped up about our Dance Club idea—not to mention bruised—that I can barely think straight.

"Oh, ladies!" Georgia calls out as class ends. "I have one small announcement, please, before you go. I just wanted to remind you that tryouts for the Limbo Central Cheerleading Squad are taking place outside on the football field on Wednesday evening at five o'clock! In addition to cheering for our awesome football and basketball teams, we also compete in Limbo-wide cheerleading competitions, and every year we put on a huge show at the end-of-year Spring Fling Carnival. It's going to be a great year, and we're looking to fill a few spots on the squad. I noticed a lot of promise today—so please come and try out!"

I don't know what hits me, but suddenly I open my mouth and this comes out: "And, if you're looking to be a part of something even cooler than cheerleading—to be part of a creative group that listens to one another and works together as a team—come join our brand-new Limbo Central Dance Club! Oh, and you don't need to try out for our club, because we're inclusive, not exclusive. If you sign up, you're in!"

If we were playing volleyball right now? That serve would have gone straight to *her* head!

Guess I need to figure out this whole starting-your-own-supernatural-club thing.

Like, now.

THE LIMBO CENTRAL CLUB MANUAL

RULE #2:

Want to start a new club? Great! All club proposals must be submitted to the administration office for official approval. Please state what your club is; why you believe it is necessary; and how it will incorporate, build, and encourage strong ghost skills. Also, please list at least one long-term goal your club will work toward achieving by the end of the year.

Chapter Two
Three's a Crowd

Lunch could not come fast enough. After my spontaneous outburst in P.E., I stopped by the administration office to find out what hoops I'll have to jump through to get this Dance Club approved. The answer? About a hundred and fifty, all of which are wrapped up neatly in the *Limbo Central Club Manual*.

Piece o'cake.

I'm so busy thinking about how to answer these club questions that I've forgotten to worry about what's going to happen at lunch. Now that Georgia is on the outs with, well, basically everyone in the group, is she going to sit somewhere else? Or is she going to stay at the regular table and make everyone feel super uncomfortable? Waiting in line for food, I realize just how awkward things could get. Seriously, who knew that being dead would be so full of real-life DRAMA?!

"What's for lunch?" a beautiful voice from behind me whispers in my ear.

Heart stops.

Butterflies flutter.

A cartoon bluebird lands on my finger. *Oh, Colin, where have you been all my afterlife? (Or, I mean, for the last day and a half.)*

"Mystery meat with a side of questionable white mush?" I answer, jokingly.

"Yum," he replies, and my knees buckle a little. "So . . . how's Limbo's new Ghostcoming Queen feeling today?"

Like she needs her King to set a date for *their* date.

STAT.

"Pretty good," I say. "It's lovely being royal."

"I'll bet."

"Hey, you don't happen to be a freakishly good dancer, do you?"

"Uhm, not last time I checked. Why?"

"Oh, nothing. It's just, I'm starting this new Dance Club with Cecily and we need members."

"Oh. Nope. Sorry," he says, putting a chocolate pudding on his tray and another one on mine without even asking.

Could he be any sweeter?!

"That's okay," I say, as we exit the kitchen and head over to our regular table.

"So, you do photography for the paper and yearbook, don't you?" I ask him.

"Yup."

"I was thinking about joining. I'm kind of into photography," I tell him, which is technically true, but it's also the most perfect way to get some alone time with Colin.

Bonus!

"Cool. If there were just a straight-up Photo Club I'd join that instead, but there isn't," he says. "I see why not, but still."

"Wait, *why* isn't there a Photo Club?"

"Well, ghost photography is tricky. We don't photograph normally."

"And that means what, exactly?"

"It's all about energy and light," he explains. "We're not physical in the same way that living people are, so the light messes with our solidity and ruins our ability to be photographed."

"So . . . you take pictures with no one in them?"

"Oh, people are *in* them, they just don't always show up when the photos develop. The strongest ones show up as holograms—basically like how you looked when you first got here. It's like a film of a person."

"Fascinating."

As we sit down, I do a quick scan of the room and see that Georgia is nowhere to be found. *Phew!* Cecily is already seated across from us. Marcus is there, too, but he's with his bandmates, Jessie Rodriguez, James Seaver, Trevor Diggs, and Miles Rennert, at the other side of the table. My only real interactions with Jessie involve his constant desire to change their band name to horrible things like Apples to Oranges or Soup Fried Rice. Every day he has another ridiculous idea. Hopefully Figure of Speech will stick! James and Trevor run the Limbo Central radio station and they DJ'd the Ghostcoming dance. Their taste in music is killer.

No pun intended.

Miles is the oldest member of the group—I think he's in his third year here. Apparently he's the one who got them the gig. I've never *actually* talked to him. He's kind of like one of my older brother's friends, you know? If I had an older brother. He's basically way too cool to be hanging out with us, and when he does it's like he's doing charity work for some cause he really believes in but knows is helpless. He's always staring into space and then quickly jotting things down on any surface he can find—a napkin, his arm, a backpack.

"Did you hear that Figure of Speech is playing at the Clairvoyance Café on Wednesday night?" Colin asks.

"Yeah, Mia told me in first period," I reply.

Cecily stays quiet.

"I'm excited to hear them," I continue. "What kind of music do they play anyway?"

"Kind of hard to say," Colin says, with a chuckle. "Guess you'll have to come and hear for yourself."

"We'll be there, right, Cece?"

"Right, Lou," she says, nonchalantly looking over in Marcus's direction. (Lou is her nickname for me.) I'm not sure if this means she's decided not to try out for cheerleading, or if she's just saying that to keep the conversation moving.

"So, what did you do on Sunday?" I ask Colin.

Please have a good excuse for not calling me! Tell me you were feeding puppies at the animal shelter or working at a soup kitchen or—

"Played, like, five hours of Xbox and napped. It was pretty stressful."

"I'll bet," I reply.

Strike One.

Cecily gives me a look that says, "I really wish he was feeding puppies!" and I want to hug her.

Just then, the March of the Cheerleaders comes into view as a group of uniform-clad girls make their way through the cafeteria single file, heading toward the table to the left of ours. I feel like I'm watching a documentary on National Geographic about how this strange species socializes in the wild. *As you can see, the female cheerleader dresses in uniform so as not to blend into her surroundings. They travel in herds so they are always on the offensive and ready to attack.*

"What's *that* all about?" I ask, curious. I know I've only been here two weeks, but I've never seen the cheerleaders wear their uniforms during the school day before, let alone do any kind of synchronized strutting or eating.

"It's one of Georgia's new ideas as captain," Colin explains. "For tryout week. She says dressing up and displaying school spirit and solidarity during lunch and school hours will help recruit new members."

Even I have to admit that's clever.

"I like our school colors," Cecily says, staring over at the cheerleaders dreamily.

"White and gray? They are sort of signature ghost colors," Colin chimes in.

"Well, they go with everything!" Cecily says, animatedly. "Even my red hair. I mean, imagine if the colors were pink and brown or something? Yuck."

So I guess she plans on wearing the uniform after all.

Just then Georgia comes over to our table and walks right up to Cecily.

"I hope you saw the message blast about cheerleading tryouts this morning," she says, putting her fake sweet on. "I think you'd be a really great addition to the team."

"Uh, thanks?" Cecily replies, but like she's asking a question.

"Hi, Colin," Georgia says, softly.

I get a twitchy feeling in my gut that makes me uncomfortable. On the one hand, if her saying a simple hello to Colin bothers me, that means I'm just as jealous and petty as she is. On the other hand, being on high alert is one hundred percent necessary, because I know this is just the beginning of her weaseling her way back into the afterlives of the people I care about. Still . . . on the other, *other* hand, I hate the idea of behaving even remotely similar to the way she would behave. But back to the other hand, I'm having a lot of trouble curbing myself right now.

Wait, how many hands *is* that?

Grrr. Emotional Girl rears her head again.

And her hands, apparently.

"Georgia," Colin says simply, acknowledging her existence. I think he's going to leave it at that and am about to feel all smug and superior when he continues. "How was the rest of your weekend? Are you doing okay?"

Strike Two.

Cecily gives me another look that says, "Just say the word and I'll make him regret knowing English!"

Obviously, not *really*. But, don't ya just love girlfriends?!

Georgia takes Colin's question as an invitation to sit down and chitchat. I think there might actually be smoke coming out of my ears and nose right now, but if I don't calm down, I'll do something weird with my ghost powers like make the mystery meat explode or turn my hair blue, so I take a few deep breaths and try to clear my mind. I need to act as if I couldn't care less that she's sitting here talking to Colin even though she's:

a) Not part of our group of friends anymore
b) Not Colin's girlfriend anymore
c) Super cruel and evil

"You and your Xbox," I hear her say, as my head reenters the conversation. She has her hand on his forearm. I stare at her hand hoping that for once my emotional ghost powers will do something useful like magically pry her ironclad grip from his arm.

Instead? Nothing happens.

"I can't help myself," Colin says. "I just love video games, man."

Man? That sounds promising . . .

"You know, we never finished that *Zombie Hunters* game we were playing last week," she says to him.

That? Does not.

Great, now she's touching his arm and playing zombie video games with him! I'm doing some Zen-type breathing, trying hard not to hang on her every word when she makes EVERYTHING so much worse.

"Maybe I can come over tonight and we can finish it? I'm so close to beating you!"

THIS? I'm gonna hang on.

Like a monkey, swinging.

How could she?! How can she possibly have the nerve to . . . and now he's just looking at her like . . .

WHAT IS HAPPENING RIGHT NOW?!

I'm eagerly awaiting Colin's response when—

"You can't!" Cecily scream-answers, overly enthusiastic.

We all turn to face her. My eyes must look like they are popping out of their sockets right now.

Because they are.

Cecily stammers, "Colin and Lucy were *just* about to agree to help me out with something top secret tonight, so, I'm afraid he's busy."

I literally have no clue what she's talking about. My brain is so confused and disjointed I can barely hear myself think, but I'm simultaneously loving her and hating her for this outburst. That's normal with best friends, right?

When no one says anything else, Georgia takes it as a sign to leave. "Well, maybe another time, then. Hope to see you at tryouts, Cecily." Then she walks back to her table.

"So, what is this top-secret thing you need our help with tonight?" Colin asks Cecily.

Now *her* eyeballs are popping out of their sockets.

"Well," she begins, "I was thinking that maybe you could get Marcus to hang out with us tonight? We could watch *Star Wars*, since you're always talking to Lucy about it—and we could have, like, a double date. What do you think?"

I can't decide if I want to hug her or shove her into a locker. What is she thinking?! I mean, she knows I'm upset that he hasn't set a date yet, and I know she's doing this to get

Georgia out of the picture, but this feels super awkward and forced. What if he thinks I put her up to it? I have to say something.

"Don't you think it'll be a little weird?" I ask her. "I mean, Colin, have you ever even hung out with Marcus alone?"

"Actually he's my roommate—"

Duh.

"And the guy I played video games with yesterday for five hours—"

Duh. Duh.

"So, yeah, I have," Colin finishes.

"Oh."

How do I not know this? I guess now that I think about it, I've never actually asked him . . .

"I didn't know you two were roommates," I continue. "Cece, did you know?"

"Marcus told me at the dance," she says.

"It's cool," Colin says, then calls out to the other side of the table. "Hey, Marcus!"

I look over at Cecily. Her cheeks are bright red with embarrassment, but the rest of her face looks like the life's been sucked out of it.

No pun intended. Again.

"*Star Wars* in the movie room later?" Colin continues, totally unconcerned. No mention of me or Cecily, or double-date movie watching of any kind. *Hmm.*

"Cool," Marcus says.

Boys!

"So," Colin says, turning back to face us, "that's solved. And just in time, too," he adds as the bell dings, signaling the end of lunch. "See you later!" he sings, and heads off to class.

I still have no idea what just happened or whether I should be happy about it. Yes, I suppose this means that tonight I kind of have a date with Colin. But is it really a date if two other people are going to be there? And does it count as him asking me out if he didn't even do the asking? Wait, correction. He *did* actually do some asking—only, the person he asked out was Marcus.

So much for being Queen to his King. Right about now? I might as well be his servant.

Hmph.

At six thirty, Cecily and I arrive at Colin and Marcus's dorm, the Dickens House, just like Colin told us, and buzz his room number. Colin's hologram pops out of the security screen.

"Be right down," he says.

"I'm nervous!" Cecily tells me. "Are you nervous?"

"I think I'm still in too much shock to be nervous," I reply. "Just calm down, it's gonna be great. Breathe."

"I'm breathing, I think," she says. "How come you're not nervous?"

"I don't know," I say, truthfully. "I guess because it doesn't really feel like a date."

"Just because it's not only the two of you? Or because you're not actually going anywhere?" she asks.

"Combo meal, I think."

"Well, it feels like a date to me," she says. "Aside from the dance, I haven't spent any time with Marcus—with or without you two."

"Hey, there," Colin says, opening the door and letting us into the building. "Did you change your outfit?" he asks me, sounding either surprised or confused. I can't tell which.

Boys. Again. Of course we changed! This is *supposed* to be a date. And, while it's kind of good that he noticed I changed (it means he's paying attention to what I look like!), now I feel weird admitting that I changed just for the date, because he clearly thinks that's not a good enough reason to change your clothes.

"Uh, yeah, well, I spilled something on myself so I didn't want to come over looking dirty."

"Or smelling!" Cecily adds. And then she just continues, like she has suddenly contracted a disease that forces her to lie uncontrollably without any filter. "It was milk, so, you know. She spilled on me, too, so then I had to change. It was a mess."

This conversation is a mess.

"Thanks for adding all those details, Cece," I say, and shoot her a look when Colin isn't facing us.

"You know you don't have to change completely when that happens. You can just clean it up ghost-style," Colin informs us. "It takes a lot of energy and skill, but I can teach you how."

"Good to know!" I say. "Probably a bit beyond us at this point, but definitely important for future klutzy moments, of which there will be many."

"I like that you're a klutz," he replies, all adorable. Suddenly I couldn't be happier that Cecily made up a fake story about me spilling milk that I didn't even drink.

"So, I thought we weren't allowed to be in your dorm?" I ask.

"You aren't allowed in our individual dorm rooms, and we're not allowed in yours," Colin says, "but every dorm has common rooms and movie rooms you can reserve for parties and stuff."

"Oh, that's cool!" I reply, starting to warm up a bit.

We head up to the third floor where it looks like all the common space is. There's a game room (which I suspect is where he and Marcus spent their Sunday), a café, the cafeteria, and a bunch of smaller social rooms. All the rooms are decorated like libraries from the eighteenth century, with lots of bookcases full of leather-bound books, leather couches, and Persian rugs. It's all very old-world English—and masculine, not that I'm surprised. Every inch of my dorm is covered with flowers.

Oh, so many flowers. But it is the Jane Austen Cottage, after all.

"So . . . where's Marcus?" Cecily asks as we head into the movie room Colin's reserved for the night.

"Good question," Colin answers. "I haven't seen him since school let out. Let me run upstairs and see if he's back yet."

Cecily and I sit down on the couches, one of us on either couch to ensure that there's room for our respective dates to sit next to us. While we wait, I try to distract us by bringing up what I've learned about starting our club. (Yes, I'll admit that the second I saw Colin, my nerves woke up from their nap.) I tell her all about the supernatural angle, and how we have to declare what the club is and what we want our end-of-year goal to be.

"So, do you have any thoughts?" I ask.

"On what, specifically?"

"Well, on any of it, really," I say. "I've been thinking about how we can incorporate the whole supernatural ghost thing into the dancing, and sure, we can float and fly and hover and add all of that into our choreography, but I don't just want to do what they do in cheerleading. We have to be different from Georgia."

"But that sounds like a lot to learn already," Cecily says. "I mean, it could take months—even longer—to learn how to incorporate that stuff into our routines."

"True. But, we'll be co-captains, so we'll be learning everything together! I was thinking that we should make our dance routines more like theater—the way we did in ballet."

"Yeah?"

"We would build the sets, the scenery, and the costumes, all with our ghost powers—AND we'd incorporate the ghost powers into the moves themselves, where it makes sense."

"That sounds cool. But also really hard. I don't think we're qualified to even do that stuff yet. I would have no idea how to."

"Jeez, Cece, don't be too encouraging or anything," I say wryly. "We'll just have to learn along the way."

"What do you think is taking them so long?" Cecily asks, anxiously.

"I don't know, but it hasn't been *that* long. Maybe they spilled some milk," I joke.

"Ha-ha. Okay, so what's our end-of-year goal?" Cecily asks.

"I think we should perform at the Spring Fling Carnival."

"What's that?"

"I'm not sure, exactly. But I know that the Cheerleading Team performs at it every year."

"So, *that's* what this is about? Can't we just leave Georgia and her Cheerleading Squad alone?"

"Don't you want our dance club to be way more awesome than her squad?"

Before Cecily can answer, Colin reappears.

"Hey, guys," Colin says, peeking his head in through the door. "I've got some bad news. Marcus isn't coming."

Can nothing in the afterlife go according to plan? First, Cecily is suddenly less-than-psyched about our Dance Club, then Marcus stands her up for their date?

This whole room is starting to smell like spilled milk.

THE LIMBO CENTRAL CLUB MANUAL

RULE #3:

Every club must have at least five members. If you are starting a new club, before you can begin the formation process you must have your first five members sign the petition (download HERE) and then hand it to your guidance counselor with the rest of the official documents when you submit your club for approval.

Chapter Three
Strike Three

"Marcus isn't coming?" I repeat, shocked. "Why not?"

"Apparently he's still practicing with the band," Colin answers, apologetically. "You know they have that gig on Wednesday night, and they only have tonight and tomorrow night to practice."

"So he just decided to stand Cecily up?" I ask, annoyed. Because that? Is not cool.

"Well, the thing is, he kind of didn't know you were going to be here."

Strike Three! We were wondering when you'd show up. So nice of you to join your siblings, Strike One and Strike Two.

"What do you mean?" I ask, even though it seems pretty self-explanatory.

"I didn't get to tell him. I figured I'd tell him when he got home from school. But then he never came home, so . . . I'm sorry, Cecily."

"It's okay," she replies, calmly. "You didn't do it on purpose."

"Are you okay?" I ask, going over to her side and putting my arm around her.

"Yeah, it's fine. No big deal," she says, sweetly. Just like Cecily.

I feel awful! She was so nervous and excited, and now she's feeling totally rejected and embarrassed. I know because girl-friends know these things. Even though feeling rejected is CRAZY, because he didn't even know she was coming, there-fore he couldn't possibly have rejected her—and right now I'm giving her a look that says exactly that! But still, she's so sad. Her face is all pouty and scrunched up like she might cry. I have to do something to cheer her up.

"I think I'm just gonna go home now," she says, quietly.

"Don't go!" Colin chimes in immediately, before I can spit out a word.

Whoa, slow your roll, tiger! You don't have to be *that* enthusiastic.

Don't get me wrong, I'm not about to send Cecily back to our room all by herself after what's just happened, but it would be nice if Colin wasn't quite as excited about her staying. I mean, this is supposed to be a date and all, isn't it? I was already on the fence about the double date, but at least that consisted of two couples. How can you have a date with three people?! What should be happening? I *should* have to twist his arm to get him to agree to let her stay and crash our date, and he should then be bummed out that he doesn't get me all to himself.

Right?

"Of course!" I cry out. "You *have* to stay and watch the movie with us. You can't go back by yourself after being stood up. Hanging with us will be much more fun! Hello—we're going to watch *Star Wars*. It's, like, the best movie ever made!" I mock to make Cecily laugh.

"Uh, I know you're kind of making fun of me right now," Colin jumps in, "but just wait till you see it. This movie will change your life."

"He's kinda right, you know," Cecily chimes in, quietly. "It's pretty good."

"*You've* seen *Star Wars*?!" I exclaim.

"Everyone's seen *Star Wars*," she says.

"Told you!" Colin blurts out, smiling, and then high-fives Cecily.

He looks giddy.

Okay, I know this shouldn't be a big deal, but he's suddenly more excited about Cecily having seen this movie than he was about us coming over to watch it in the first place. It's like he's just realized he was actually going to have fun because she's here. Ugh. I hate this. Why do I feel like every girl in Limbo has more in common with him than I do right now? First, Georgia, with her video-game playing, now Cecily, with *Star Wars*. Am I missing something? I thought we really connected before, but I don't know, maybe I was wrong. Maybe this is just going to be a total epic fail.

Worst. First. Date. Ever.

"Well, Lucy's gonna love it, too," Cecily adds, thoughtfully. "This is the kind of thing she's into. I mean, I literally have to beg to get her to go see anything romantic, or anything that doesn't involve some kind of fight for world domination."

"Right, Cece," I say, smiling at Colin. "You wanna battle aliens and kill zombies, I'm your gal."

Hint, hint.

"Good to know," he replies, coming to sit next to me on the couch.

I shoot Cecily a smile. Even though the date she was crazy excited for got canceled, like, while she was on it, she's still with it enough to have my back while my date is still going.

Girlfriends rock.

"So, Cecily, are you a surfer, too?" Colin asks.

"Not really," she replies. "I went with Lucy and Felix a couple of times, but I'm more of a skiing girl. My family would go every winter."

"Me too!" Colin tells her, a look of awe and surprise on his face. "I'm a snowboarder, but I love it all."

Not that I'm keeping score or anything, but . . .

Georgia	Cece	Me
• ex-gf advantage • zombie video game advantage	• Star Wars advantage • snow sports advantage	• photography? • forced date
2 points	2 points	-1 point

Feels like the strikes are starting to pile up against *me* this time.

"Next, Lucy's gonna teach me how to surf, right, dude?" Colin says, knocking my arm with his elbow lightly.

I can't tell if he's actually calling me dude (*vom!*) or if he's saying it ironically.

"Surf's up!" I reply, half sarcastic just in case.

"So, should we put on the movie?" he asks.

Cecily and I both nod.

The lights go out and the movie starts, and all I can think about is whether or not he's going to try to hold my hand. I know it's silly. It's our first not-even-a-date date and we're not alone, so he probably wouldn't hold my hand now even if he wanted to. And let's just be honest: The jury is still out on whether he wants to. Right now? It seems his emotions are all over the place like pinballs in a machine, and I'm trying desperately to sink a ball—any ball!—and failing miserably.

Worst. Game. Ever.

For almost two hours, we stare at the screen watching the movie, and nothing happens except that Cecily and Colin keep going off about what characters they like the most and what their favorite parts are. At this point, I'm almost itching to go home when Marcus walks in the room.

"Hey! I didn't know you guys were gonna be here! Hi, Cecily," he says, excitedly. "I would have ditched the band if I knew that—dude, why didn't you text me back?"

"Text him?" I exclaim. "Ghosts can have cell phones?"

"They're actually more like mini Tabulators, but kind of," Colin corrects me. "It's called a Tabby. New students don't get them until they pass the probation period and first tactical exam. It's, like, three months, I think."

"Cool," I say, momentarily distracted by the excitement of one day having a phone-like thing again! (I've been going through WITHDRAWAL like nobody's business.)

"So, dude, why didn't you text me back?" Marcus presses.

"I just figured with the gig coming you needed to practice."

"Yeah . . . you're right, we did," Marcus agrees. "It's sounding pretty tight, though."

"That's good," Cecily says, perking up and joining the conversation.

"You have to come hear us play on Wednesday!" he tells her, enthusiastically.

I try to give Colin a look that says, "Aww, how cute are they!" But he doesn't look back at me. He's staring intently at Cecily and Marcus talking, and either he's purposely not looking at me or he's lost in a trance. I can't tell if he's mad or confused or just tired, but these pinballs have gone completely rogue.

R.O.G.U.E.

"So you'll come, right? It's at six at the Clairvoyance Café," Marcus asks again, waiting eagerly for Cecily's reply.

"Yes, of course we'll be there," she says. "I mean, I have cheerleading tryouts at five, but it shouldn't take more than an hour."

"Sweet. Then we can hang out after the set. I'll make it up to you for standing you up tonight—even though that was totally Colin's bad."

"Sounds like a plan!" she says, smiling.

See, Colin? That's how it's done.

1. Find the girl you like.
2. Ask her out on a date.
3. PICK the day and time.

How is it possible that this situation has gotten so ridiculously and utterly complicated? I've been obsessing over Colin for the last two weeks—yes, I admit it. Obsessing. Thinking about our first date and how amazing it's going to be, and then it finally comes (even if it did involve him asking out a boy instead of me), and it falls completely and totally flat. Is it me? Have I done something to turn him off? Why do I feel like I didn't pass the test?

Full-on cry face.

Conclusion? Either Colin comes from a galaxy far, far away, or I do.

"So, do you want to join our new Dance Club?" I ask Briana Clark the next day at school, between fifth and sixth periods. Chloe already signed up and she thinks Briana will be game, too.

"What kind of dance?" she asks me, staring at me with her chocolate-brown eyes, her hands pulling and separating her thick curls. "I'm not into anything weird like modern or interpretive dance."

A girl after my own heart.

"Nah, none of that. It's going be more contemporary, like storytelling to pop music."

"Sounds fun! Count me in. As long as it doesn't interfere with Cheerleading."

"That's a concern for lots of people, so I'm already accounting for it. I'm so excited to have you aboard—welcome to the Limbos!"

"That's a cute name," Chloe says. "Are we going to have to wear uniforms?"

"I don't think so, unless that's something people want. But I figure our costumes are going to change based on performances, so uniforms would only be for practice—and I don't think that's really necessary, do you? People should be able to express themselves by wearing whatever they want."

"You're, like, the exact opposite of Georgia," Briana says, with a chuckle.

Chloe smirks. She told me I would like Briana, and so far, she's right.

"Good," I reply. "That's what I'm going for."

Just then the bell rings, and we three part ways. With four signatures on my petition, I'm just one shy of being able to officially get this club submitted. I wonder if Cecily's had any luck getting members, but she's probably too distracted by the Cheerleading tryouts to be thinking about our club. The truth is? I'm kind of bummed. I expected her to be way more jazzed about this. But she acts so aloof and disconnected every time the subject of Dance Club comes up. It's like someone else invaded her body.

Missing friend alert.

Like today? She got up at the crack of dawn to go practice her routine for Wednesday. And at lunch, when I asked her if she would show it to me she told me she wasn't ready for me to see it yet. Not ready yet! Cecily and I have been dancing together since we were, like, five. There's never been a moment when she's been too embarrassed to try something in front of me. We are constantly helping one another—telling each other what we're doing wrong—especially when we're trying out advanced combinations or new choreography. *Drop your hip. Lower your arm. Square your shoulders.* These phrases left our mouths as often as air went into them. Now she's suddenly shy? With cheerleading, of all things?

There's something strange in the air lately, and it's making my throat itch.

At the end of eighth period, I meet up with Colin to get the lowdown on this photography business. He asked me during lunch if I wanted to take some pictures after school, and even though last night was kind of a bust, I can't say I wasn't excited when he suggested a new outing. It's not *exactly* a date, but it's progress. And since Cecily is working on her routine now anyway without my help, it's nice to have my own hobby to distract me. Plus, it seems to be the one thing Colin and I have in common these days.

"You ready to get your photo on?" Colin says, materializing next to my locker sporting a big smile.

"Totally. But where do I get a camera?"

"You don't. I mean, you have to create one yourself, but

that's really advanced. Unless you have, like, two hundred dollars to drop on a pre-made one."

"Pass."

"That's what I thought. So, making one is the only way, but like I said, it's advanced energy creation. You'd have to account for different amounts and types of energy so that the pictures reflect exactly what you snapped and all that. It took me, like, four months to make mine."

"Wow, that's intense," I reply. "Okay, but if everything is made out of energy, why can't we just doctor the pictures when people don't show up in them?" I ask, confused.

"You can, technically, but that's not the process of photography, is it? It's like using Photoshop."

"But aren't you just re-creating what was really there?"

"Not necessarily. There are a lot of things the camera would capture that the mind wouldn't think of. Also, why don't we show up?! I want to fix that—not just draw over it."

"I see your point," I say, and I mean it.

"You can borrow my camera for now, if you'd like."

"Thanks! So, what's the plan?"

"Let's get out of here. There's a spooky old barn a little ways north that's full of cool photo ops."

"Spooky?" I repeat, with a laugh. "How? Is it haunted with *living* people?"

"Be careful what you joke about," he replies, all dark and stormy, and then gives me a wink.

We hop on the bus heading north, away from the center of town, where school and all the stores and shops are. We sit next to each other, and stare out the window at the scenery silently. It's breathtaking. We exit the main town and laid out before us are wheat fields and farmland as far as the eye can see, with gorgeous grayish-white mountain peaks way off in the distance. After a while, you stop noticing all the energy measurements hanging above everything and just get lost in how pretty it all is. Every few acres there's a house.

Even though we're not speaking, I can feel Colin look at me occasionally, and every couple of minutes his knee brushes up against mine, or his hand accidentally slides closer to me. I can feel my insides start to tighten and loosen at the same time, like the perfect grilled-cheese sandwich: the bread is crispy and toasted, but the inside, all gooey and melted, is dripping over the edges.

Ooh, now I'm hungry.

Just when I think his hand is finally going to make contact with mine, the bus comes to a halt and he pulls his hand away. My delicious grilled-cheese sandwich of emotions feels like it's been dropped in cold water. In my frustration, I accidentally send my book bag cascading across the floor, like a hockey puck, until it slams against the back of the bus in anger.

Get a grip, girl.

"Was that you, or the bus?" he asks, standing up.

I'm positive it was me, but I lie. (A teeny, tiny, little white lie never hurt anyone, right?)

"I think it was the bus."

"Right. This is us," he says, heading to the front to exit.

The barn is about a half-mile walk from the bus stop. When we get there, I see exactly why he says it's spooky. It's really big and full of weird stuff because it's abandoned. Like it's a storage place for a garage sale that hasn't happened yet, and probably never will. We enter the barn, and I immediately feel a warm breeze wash over me, like I've just stepped into a mild sauna. There's a weird energy about this place. I have a flashback of being back home with my family, watching TV, the smell of freshly popped popcorn and scent of my grandmother's blanket that we always snuggled under on the couch.

"You okay?" Colin asks.

I snap out of my daze. "Yeah, I'm fine, thanks."

"Cool. So, you ready to be my subject?" he asks. "I'll show you what I mean about photos being tricky."

"Pose me, boss!"

He sets me up in an old rocking chair and then positions some objects next to me, to help demonstrate his point. There's a red wooden crate with some old dolls in it, a lamp, a yellow-and-white basket, and a stack of old books. I wonder if Colin thinks I'm pretty as he looks through his viewfinder to snap the perfect shot. I can't help but think about Georgia. She might be awful, but she's also really pretty. (Pretty awful. Ha.) But really, her chic black hair and bright blue eyes—she's like a model. What is he thinking when he looks at me? I stare at him, hoping to somehow telepathically read him, even though in Beginner's Telepathy you only learn theory, not practice. Once again I can feel my body heating up, all my energy is being drawn to my heart like a magnet.

"Okay," he says, "Come and see for yourself. I bet you won't even show up as a shadow since you're such new energy."

I get up and walk over to him. He switches the camera from snapping mode to playback mode, and the last picture he took appears on the screen.

And there I am, perfectly sharp, and looking almost solid.

His eyebrows scrunch up like he's confused, and he flips back through more of the shots he took for confirmation. Shot after shot after shot.

I appear in every single one. Some are stronger than others, but I'm there. Always.

"I don't understand," he says, flabbergasted. "I've literally never seen this happen before."

"I don't know what to say," I reply. Because I don't.

"You're amazing!" he sings, with a huge smile on his face. "You're my muse!"

His muse?

Uhm . . . I guess I just sank the pinball?

To: Ms. Cecily Vanderberg
From: Ms. Georgia Sinclaire

You're Invited!

It's that time of year again, so whip out your party shoes and get ready for my Happy Ghostday Bash!

Let's celebrate the day I crossed over into the afterlife in style at The Cove on the beach with a bonfire, killer DJ, BBQ, and, of course, dancing.

Gifts aren't necessary, but they will be appreciated. ☺

7 p.m., The Cove (off of Death Row Ave.)
Saturday, October 31

Georgia Sinclaire

Chapter Four
Word on the Street

Wednesday morning at school feels like déjà vu of my first day as a ghost. Everyone is staring at me in the hallway with these shocked expressions, as if someone posted a video of me eating out of the garbage (which, for the record, I've NEVER done) or picking something out of my ears (which, okay, I *have* done . . . but who hasn't?!) without my knowledge, and they've all been frantically gabbing about it behind my back.

Whispers fill the air as I walk to my locker from fourth period. "What is *with* everyone?" I say to Cecily.

"You didn't hear?" she asks. "Apparently everyone is talking about your magical ghostly powers that allow you to show up in photos so easily."

"How do you know that?"

"Colin told me in Ghost Hunters last period."

"Oh."

As we make our way to the cafeteria for lunch, my mind runs amuck. It never bothered me before that they have a class together, but now I'm starting to wonder . . . what if they become, like, friends? What if they get even closer than he is with me? Or worse, what if he starts liking her as more than a friend and they start dating and I turn into a total loser weirdo with crazy powers who no one wants anything to do with!!

"Lou, what's going on in your head right now?"

"Nothing, why?" I remark, a little too quickly.

"Because your hair just turned bright green."

Unbelievable. Green with envy? Hardy-har-har, ghost powers. I dash into the bathroom and lock myself in a stall. Concentrating on breathing out the bad feelings and calming my nerves, I close my eyes and think of the ocean waves coming in and out, me and Felix riding A-frames and barrels till the sun sets. After a couple of minutes, I open my eyes and look down to find that my hair has transformed back to its natural color. All is normal again.

For now.

We get food and head over to our usual table. The cheerleaders are back in uniform sitting at the table next to us.

Tryouts are tonight, so hopefully this means we won't have to see them suited up again tomorrow, but with Georgia, anything is possible. She could make this a permanent thing for all I know. I notice that Cecily and Georgia keep exchanging looks, ping-ponging back and forth, back and forth. I'm getting dizzy just watching.

"What's up with you and Georgia? Why do you keep staring at each other?"

"What? We're not!" Cecily says, immediately self-conscious. "I wasn't looking at her specifically—just, you know, the squad in general."

"Okay, then why is *she* looking at you?"

"She's not. I think she's just looking over here, you know, because . . . well, you know why."

I don't actually know why, but I don't ask.

"Whatever," I reply, openly irritated.

"What's the matter with you?" she whispers in my ear, so no one else can hear. "Why are you being so snippy?"

I lean in close. "I'm sorry, it's just . . . nothing is going the way it's supposed to go. Georgia was supposed to disappear after Ghostcoming, and Colin and I were supposed to go on a date, and you and I were supposed to start our Dance Club. None of it's working out the right way."

"Well, I hate to break it to you, Lou, but Georgia's never going to just go away," Cecily says, quietly.

"And?"

"And . . . things with Colin will sort themselves out?" she says shakily, but I can tell she doesn't really believe it.

Still, I have bigger issues than Colin to deal with right now, so I let that go.

"And what about the Limbos?" I prod.

"That'll happen, too. Maybe not as quickly as you want it to, but you'll make it work—I know you will."

I pay close attention to how Cecily leaves herself out of the Dance Club equation. *You'll* make it work. Not *we'll* make it work. She's got her eye on a different prize. If her secret eye conversation with Georgia is any indication of what's to come, her top—and possibly only—priority is winning the white-and-gray pleated skirt and too-tight crop top that says LIMBO CHEER SQUAD on the back. And I have absolutely no idea what to do about it.

"So . . . then you're *not* going to tell me about the ghost-day party invitation Georgia specifically sent to you and not me?" I ask, trying not to sound too bitter.

"Of course I was going to tell you!" she cries out. "Just not right now. I was going to wait until we were alone, and you were less irritable."

"I'm not irritable, I'm annoyed."

Before she can reply, Colin, Mia, and Trey show up, and Trey calls out, "So, Lucy, I hear changing your appearance isn't your only super ghost power."

Mia squeezes in next to me and gives me a wink. "Super ghost power is right—you are *wearing* that outfit, girlfriend."

We both chuckle, and in that moment I'm so happy she's here. The conversation with Cecily is definitely heading into THE BAD PLACE, and Mia's laid-back, chill attitude is exactly what we need to diffuse it.

"Word on the street has it you have the magical ability to be photographed," Trey continues his original train of thought.

"Word on the street?" I say, laughing at him.

"Dude, WORD ON THE STREET!" Jessie suddenly calls out from a few seats down. "*That* should be our band name!"

"NO!" literally everyone at the table screams at once.

This is followed by several minutes of extreme uncontrollable laughter while Jessie looks at all of us like we've just shaved his cat. I would be offended that he wants to change the band name if I wasn't so busy laughing my head off.

Things finally calm down, and suddenly it's quiet again.

"So, did everyone get the invite to Georgia's bash?" Mia asks.

There's a flash of nods across the table, and it becomes clear pretty quickly that I'm the only one who wasn't invited.

The cheese stands alone.

Colin and Mia are both staring at me like I might lose my lunch any second now. Or maybe they're worried I might do something unruly to *Georgia's* lunch . . . Either way, they are both eyeing me like two very concerned doctors in a mental institution.

"Can you both stop looking at me like that?" I plead. "I'm fine, I promise!"

I'm trying my best to be upbeat. I don't want them all feeling sorry for me; I'm *not* a charity case. If they want to go to some mean girl's ghostday party, so be it! I'm not standing in anyone's way.

Cecily remains silent, staring down at her hands intently, as if she's gearing up for some kind of hand-modeling Olympics and can't be bothered to partake in the conversation.

"I wouldn't go to her party even if she invited me," I remind them, "so no harm done."

"But still, it's just . . . mean," Mia says, almost like she's disappointed in Georgia. As if this is somehow surprising.

Now Colin is staring down at his hands. Where are we? The Limbo Central Hand Convention!?

"It's really okay," I say calmly, getting up from the table.

"Where are you going?" Colin asks, suddenly able to wrestle his eyes away from his award-worthy hands.

"I just remembered I have to go ask Ms. Keaner something, about the Dance Club stuff. I'll see you all later."

I get up and get out of there as quickly as I can. I don't know where I'm going—not too far because it's only lunchtime and I still need to finish the school day—but I need some fresh air.

Like, now.

I end up out on the playground and slump down on a swing. I know they're meant for little kids, but I still love them. Something about being up in the air . . . When I was young, it always felt about as close to being able to fly as humanly possible. But that was before. Now I'm a ghost, and flying is basically our easiest and first mode of transport.

But I don't know, floating just doesn't feel the same.

I start thinking about everything that's happened since the Ghostcoming dance, and I don't know whether to laugh or cry. Probably laugh, because I still haven't figured out how to produce tears yet, and let's be real, crying without tears is

WAY less satisfying. It's just . . . everything that could go wrong has, like my afterlife has been put into one of those trash compactor machines and is being crushed from all sides. Winning Ghostcoming Queen was supposed to be this symbol that the Georgias of the school don't get to rule anymore—that they don't always get what they want. But Georgia is like some kind of superhero. No matter how many times I knock her down, she's just going to get right back up, isn't she? I have this vision of playing Whack-a-Mole at the arcade, but instead of the mole popping up it's Georgia's face with a speech bubble that says, "Georgia Lives 4Ever!"

Which is ironic, since she's dead.

I feel myself get more and more heated, and so does the swing—it's currently hovering around 180 degrees high, which is already higher than I ever went as a child, and I'm not even sure how it's physically possible.

I try to calm myself down.

But my mind wanders . . .

Colin's another epic fail. I mean, after the dance we were supposed to be on our way to cute coupledom Lady-and-the-Tramp-style. It was finally going to be *my* turn to have a boyfriend. Or at least a first date! But that all went sour, too, didn't it? Does Colin want me to be his girlfriend or some photographic specimen he's studying? And Cecily? I don't even know what to say about her. I thought that this Dance Club was something we were going to share together, kind of like old times. But now she's drooling over the cheerleading uniforms, getting party invitations and not telling me about them, and basically showing, like, zero interest in the Limbos. Next thing I know she's going to end up helping Georgia throw the very party that I'm not invited to!

I should say something to her about how I'm feeling, but what am I going to say? "I hate that you're thinking of joining the Cheerleading Squad and I don't want you to go to Georgia's party?" I mean, Georgia completely threw Cecily under the bus at the dance, just to get me in trouble! Doesn't that mean anything to her anymore, or have the pom-poms totally obstructed her view of reality?

But I can't say any of these things. Because saying them, that would be so . . . harsh. And I don't want to fight.

I get so worked up that my swing starts flying higher and higher in the air—more than 180 degrees, and now I *know* this isn't physically possible. Well, not normally, anyway. When I was younger, my brother, Sammy, and I used to play that game on the swings in our backyard—how high can you go? We'd stretch our legs out really long and try to touch the clouds with our feet. *That* was fun.

This is not.

"Ahhhhhh!" I screech as I lose complete control.

What else is new.

My swing climbs higher and higher until I end up looping it all the way up, over, and around the pole, like my own mini rollercoaster.

Crazy ghost energy.

When I've recovered from my circus moves and managed to slow down a bit, I shift over to the next swing, so I'm not hanging ten feet above the ground, and try to act like I had nothing to do with the swing wraparound. That's when I notice Cecily walking across the playground, heading toward me. She sits down on the other normal-height swing next to mine.

We're basically just rocking back and forth, kicking the dirt.

"I'm sorry you didn't get invited to Georgia's party," she says.

"I'm not," I reply. I'm not cold, exactly, but I'm not cheery, either.

"I know you don't want me to go," she tells me.

Of course I don't want her to go, but I don't admit it. Instead, I say, "I would never tell you what to do or not do."

What I want to say is that we swore we would always have each other's backs. We promised we'd be there for one another no matter what. We said we were best friends, and that being in Limbo meant we had a shot at a friendship do-over—so we could do things differently than we did before when ballet was all-consuming and every girl was always out for herself. What I want to say is, "Doesn't that mean anything to you anymore?"

But I don't.

"The only reason I would go is if I get onto the squad," she says, after what feels like a long pause. "I'll have to go, if that happens, you know, to support her and the team."

"Right."

"I just . . . I don't think it's fair for me to have to give up what I want because you have issues with Georgia. It's not like she and I are going to become friends or anything. It's all about the squad."

"Okay, whatever you say."

Just then the bell rings, signaling the end of lunch.

"Well, we better go to class," she says.

We both get up and walk toward the back entrance of the school. Neither of us says anything else.

I don't know what to feel anymore. Maybe she's right? Maybe I'm making too big a deal out of this, and it's not about me and my thing with Georgia. Maybe I need to be more supportive of Cecily? Isn't that what best friends are supposed to do? I feel all turned around. My brain is a soup of opposing thoughts and emotions, none of which taste good together.

This soup? Is inedible.

When the last bell of the day rings, I look for Cecily by her locker, but she's not there. I figure she's somewhere practicing for tryouts in a couple of hours, so I head to the gym to see if she's there and . . .

Ding! Ding! Ding!

She's just about to start running through her moves, and I don't want to disturb her or ruin her mojo. So I stand outside and peek through the windows on the double doors.

And what I see? Blows my mind!

She's really good. She's jumping up and down, cheering, but keeping her technique the whole time—which is super hard—and she's doing some CRAZY gymnastics moves.

Like, seventeen flips in a row across the gym floor. At one point she does a standing backflip!

Standing. Backflip.

What the what?!

I burst into the gym and yell, "Uh, excuse me, but how did you get so insanely amazing at this and why don't I know that you can do a million backflips in a row? Why don't I know that you can do *one* backflip?!"

"You scared me!" she screams. "What are you doing here?"

"I'm here to help you practice for tryouts."

"But . . . do you really think it was good?"

"Please tell me you're joking. That? Was awesome. You're way better than everyone on the squad—including Black Mop Head."

"Who?" Cecily says, with a laugh.

"That's Georgia's new nickname. You like it?"

"It's very creative," she says, wiping the sweat off her face with a towel.

"So, how come you never told me you could do gymnastics?"

"I guess it never really came up. Also, it's sort of taboo to do gymnastics if you're into ballet, you know. People get all judge-y about which is better."

Instinctually I say, "Uh, ballet, obviously."

"See?"

"Right, sorry. Well, you're über-talented. Georgia's gonna flip."

"What happened to Black Mop Head?"

"Oh whoops! I guess it's gonna take some getting used to. It's hard to remember."

"And long. It sounds like an appliance."

"Call this number for the Black Mop Head Three Thousand—with a head that actually swivels all the way around!"

We both start laughing, and it seems like the ice is finally thawing.

We stay in the gym until tryouts, hanging out and talking, and of course going over her routine. I help her add some ghostly additions like hovering in the air or floating instead of jumping to show them that she understands cheerleading is a little different up here. She's still pretty new to the ghost thing, so I doubt she'll be required to do anything fancy from the start. I'm pretty sure that Georgia already has her mind set on having Cecily join the squad no matter how good or bad she is, but since Cece rocks, it's a no-brainer.

Five o'clock rolls around and we head out to the football

field. I sit in the bleachers and watch. Don't get me wrong, I still think Black Mop Head is the bane of my afterlife and I'm still on high alert about how this whole Cecily-on-the-squad scenario is going to play out. And the whole Limbos thing? That's another situation entirely. But Cecily's right about this—my beef with Black Mop Head (it just rolls off the tongue now!) shouldn't play into whether or not Cece gets to follow her passion and do something that makes her happy. I have to accept it and learn to live with it, and support Cecily. That's what best friends do, right?

"Thank you all for coming to tryouts for the Limbo Cheerleading Squad!" Georgia says, perky and enthusiastic. "I'm so excited to see how many new faces are here to try out. Just one important thing to note before we begin: Because the squad needs to be healthy and available to support the Limbo football and basketball teams all year round, and we don't want to run the risk of anyone getting hurt or having scheduling conflicts, if you become a member of the Cheerleading squad you will *not* be allowed to participate in any other sports-related clubs."

Rah. Rah. Rah.

Sis. Boom. AHHHHHHHHHHHHHH!

THE
LIMBO CENTRAL
CLUB MANUAL

RULE #4:

Every club must appoint a captain or
president. Keep in mind, this is a serious
job that requires dedication, commitment,
sensitivity, and a firm hand. Please be
sure to understand what is involved before
deciding to take on this pivotal role.

Chapter Five
Georgia 2.0

Georgia Black Mop Head McScary just voided half of my Limbos club members—and I only had four to begin with! If there's ever a moment for my emotions to get the better of me and go nuts on someone, this is it.

Ready. Set. Go.

Now because of her stupid rule, I have to cross Briana and Chloe off the list. And who knows what's going to happen with Cecily . . . She was *supposed* to be my co-captain! I know before it seemed like she already had her foot halfway out the door, but after what happened in the gym earlier I thought we were back on track. I told her I want her to be happy, and when I watched her in the gym doing all her incredible flips and stuff? She did look happy. So I'm totally supportive of her being on the squad now. I mean, I'm sitting here up in the bleachers cheering her on, aren't I?

Of course Cecily completely kills her audition. There's no question that she's getting an invitation to join. The only question is whether or not she'll accept it now that the rules have changed.

"Thank you again to everyone who showed up!" Georgia calls out.

It's 5:50 P.M., and Figure of Speech is about to go on. We'll make it just in the nick of time.

"If I call out your name, you've been accepted onto the squad. If I don't, keep practicing and come try out again next year!"

She runs down a list of names in alphabetical order, most of which I don't recognize, and finally she ends with—

"Cecily Vanderberg!"

I walk down from the bleachers and go over to congratulate Cecily, but this new rule has made it significantly more challenging for me to fake a smile.

The thing is, before it became an issue of choosing one or the other, Cecily was right: I needed to set my anti-Georgia movement aside and be a good friend. If Cecily was willing to do both Cheerleading squad and Dance Club, why should I have had a problem with it? But now that Georgia has made it about choosing—and make no mistake, she's doing this on purpose—things are different. Georgia's changing the rules.

"I guess congratulations are in order," I say, giving Cecily a hug.

"Yeah," she says. "Thanks."

"Did you know about the no-other-sports-clubs rule?" I ask.

"No, it's news to me," she says. "But there's still a lot I don't know. Maybe there's a way around it? Like, maybe I can talk to Ms. Keaner or something?"

"I don't think Georgia could have made that kind of rule without getting approval," I say. "It looks like you're going to have to choose between Georgia and me."

"Don't say that," she says. "Don't make me choose, it's not fair."

"*I'm* not making you choose—I came here to support you, remember? Georgia is making you choose. She's doing this on purpose, you know that, right?"

"Maybe she is. But *she's* making me choose between Cheerleading and Dance Club; *you're* making me choose between her and you."

"Is there really a difference?" I ask, shocked.

Just then some of the girls on the squad call out to Cecily.

"We're going to go to the Spooky Soda Shoppe to celebrate with some of the football players. It's a tradition after tryouts. You want to come?"

"Sure!" she calls back to them.

"What about Marcus and Figure of Speech?" I ask her. "They're going on, like, now."

"I'll just . . . I'll meet you there in a bit."

So *that's* how it is.

I speed over to the Clairvoyance Café, trying to not think about everything that just happened. When I see that the band is still warming up, I breathe a sigh of relief that I'm not late. Maybe Cecily won't miss much, either.

I walk over to the counter to order something to drink but before I say anything the girl behind the register announces, "That'll be $5.25."

"But I—"

"One medium hot chocolate with whipped cream and a chocolate-chip biscotti for here, right? That'll be $5.25."

Whoa, they really are clairvoyant, aren't they? This is the second order of mine that they've gotten right before I even opened my mouth. I wonder if they're ever wrong . . .

"No, we're never wrong," she says, handing me my goodies. "Enjoy!"

"You should really take this on the road," I say, and head over to the table where Mia and Trey are sitting.

As I walk, I scan the room and notice about fifteen other kids from school, but I don't know any of them by name. Colin is nowhere to be found. And then it occurs to me: The cheerleaders said they were going to celebrate with some of the football players—that it was a tradition? And Colin is a football player.

Ugh.

Did Colin and Cecily really ditch their friends' first gig for an outing at the Spooky Soda Shoppe? How is a group of football players and cheerleaders eating ice cream a tradition, anyway? Tradition is dressing up for Halloween. Tradition is opening presents on Christmas morning. Tradition is getting your license when you turn sixteen!

This? Is lame.

I reach the table and slump down in my chair, annoyed.

"Hey, Lucy, what's up?" Mia asks, cautiously. "What's the matter? And where's Cecily?"

"Out celebrating her descent into the underworld," I say. I take a sip of my hot chocolate. It's warm and delicious, and it's the only thing putting a smile on my face.

"Should I know what that means?" Mia asks, cautiously.

"Don't you know about the *famous* post-cheerleading try-outs tradition of eating ice cream in front of football players? I mean, it's just so . . . traditional! And you know traditions cannot be broken."

"Oh . . . *that*."

I'm about to go off on Colin, too, when the band starts playing. After a few seconds, I'm already engrossed and bopping along to the beat. They're actually good! Really good. Their sound is a mix of indie rock and electronic pop—not at all what I was expecting.

After a little while, my eye catches Miles Rennert and I can't look away. He's rocking out on the keyboard and lead vocals, and it's making me swoon. I mean, they are all talented, but Miles is different. He's completely lost in the music. Like it's hypnotizing him, or something.

Whatever it is? It's adorable.

"Are you upset that Colin isn't here?" Mia whispers in my ear.

Colin *who*? (Just kidding. Unfortunately.)

"Nah, it's fine. If he'd rather be out with cheerleaders than here with me listening to his friends play an awesome set, then maybe we aren't meant to be after all."

After about twenty minutes, Colin materializes in a chair next to mine.

Not literally. (I don't think . . .)

"I thought you were off partaking in some football ritual?" I say, without turning to face him.

"It's tradition for the football team to welcome the new cheerleaders to the squad. I *had* to stop by for a few minutes."

"Right," I reply.

"Don't be mad. I'm here now," he says, smiling, squeezing my arm.

"I'm not mad. It's not like we planned to come here together or anything."

He stays silent.

I can't tell if I'm being mean or not, and isn't that something one should be able to figure out? The truth is we *didn't* agree to come here together, so technically it's not like he owes it to me to be here on time. Or to even come in the first place, actually. Things between us are so strange at this point that I'm not sure he owes me anything at all. He's not my tutor anymore. We don't seem to be anything more than friends.

But I'm definitely annoyed. I guess I just expected more from him.

I feel my face getting red, and before I accidentally do anything crazy, like pour what's left of my hot chocolate over his head, I change the subject.

"Hey, did you bring your camera? I'd love to take some shots of the band."

"Sure," he says, and hands it to me.

I head over to the side of the stage, crouch down, and start shooting. Even though I'm supposed to be photographing the whole band, I keep gravitating toward Miles. His dark brown curls are kind of bobbing up and down to the beat, and when the light hits him just right I can see the sweat glistening on his face. It must be really hot up there under all those spotlights. He notices me and gives me a little nod and a smile. I lose my balance and fall over.

Why am I acting like a crushed-out fangirl right now? I mean, I still like Colin. I know I still like Colin by the amount of anger that flushed through my veins when I realized that he was hanging out with Georgia and Cecily instead of being here—with me. And Miles is pretty much the most unattainable guy at Limbo. First of all, he's, like, three years older than me. Second, he's like . . . just . . . well, look at him? He's basically five seconds away from being a famous musician. There's no way he's interested in me.

"Hey," Colin calls to me in between songs. "Let's see what you've got so far."

I head back to my seat and offer him his camera. He flips through the shots, and I turn back to the band.

"Unbelievable!"

"What?" I say, facing him again.

"Looks like you have some kind of energy flowing between you and Miles," he says.

"What do you mean? What are you talking about?" I shoot back, embarrassed and nervous. "I barely even know Miles!"

"The pictures?" Colin says, confused. "He's the only one showing up in them. But he's, like, totally solid."

"I thought *I'm* the only one who shows up solid in pictures." I say, taking back the camera to see for myself. He's right. Shot after shot after shot is just Miles, up on stage. Solid as a living being.

"Apparently not. Maybe your power doesn't just come out in front of the camera," Colin says. "Maybe you're powerful behind it, too."

I try to remember what was going through my head when I took those photos. Then it hits me. Sure enough, my emotion meter was on high when I was shooting Miles. That's always when weird things happen, isn't it? Except this time I didn't send any coffees flying halfway across the room or make the keys on his keyboard pop off. I made him show up in pictures! This is about the only cool thing Emotional Girl has going for her.

Round of applause.

"Remember that day at the beach, like, my first week here, when you were tutoring me and my mind drew that heart in the sand out of nowhere?" I ask Colin.

"Uh, yeah," he says, smiling. "That would be hard to forget."

"Well, that kind of thing tends to happen. A lot. You don't even see the half of it."

"Okay . . . what does that have to do with anything?"

"Just that, unfortunately, the emotions running around inside me often come out in strange, ghostly accidents. And I think this whole photo thing is one of them. Only this isn't a disaster like the rest of the things that happen. This is actually, well, awesome."

"So you're telling me that you can harness the energy of your emotions and translate that into light?"

"I don't know, maybe?" I reply, confused. "I'm telling you that my hyperemotional state of being that is usually the death of me seems to be the reason why I can take good photos and appear in photos and other people can't. It's like a whiny superpower."

"Ha-ha," Colin laughs. "I like that."

When the song ends, Marcus gets on the microphone. "Thank you so much for coming to hear us play—this is going to be our final song. Once again, we're Figure of Speech."

I can't believe it's already been an hour since they started.

Marcus looks over at our table. I know he's searching the crowd for Cecily. I feel awful. She promised him that she'd be here, and they were going to have their first date after the set. Ironically, this date was supposed to make up for him standing her up on Monday night, which he technically didn't even do! And now Cecily is doing the same exact thing to him, only this time? She's doing it on purpose.

They start playing their last song, and I feel Colin's hand brush up against mine under the table. I look at him, and he takes my hand and smiles. The dimple on his left cheek comes out, and I feel my head involuntarily lean to the side, like I'm suddenly too weak to hold it upright. Colin is finally holding my hand.

Heart racing.

"You know, I thought that drawing in the sand that

day was really cute," he says. "I was already starting to like you then."

Panic setting in.

At that moment the door opens and Cecily, Georgia, Chloe, and Briana come waltzing in with Jonah Abbot, Trey's older brother, and a couple of other football players. I jump a little and drop Colin's hand.

I can't tell if I did it on purpose or by mistake, but I don't pick it up again.

When the band finally finishes, we all applaud extra loudly and scream for an encore, but they don't do one.

Cecily appears beside our table. "So, how were they?" she asks, all cheerful, like there's absolutely nothing wrong with her showing up an hour late.

I don't answer.

"They were really good," Trey says, filling the awkward silence.

"Cool, I'm sorry I missed it."

"Marcus *was* looking for you," I say, because I can't help myself.

"I'm sure he'll understand," she snaps back, and gives me a look that says, "Back off."

What is going on here? How did *I* become the bad guy? All of a sudden Cecily decides that it's okay to choose enemies over friends and go back on promises and stand up really nice guys, and *I'm* the one who gets the cold shoulder? Who died and made her Georgia 2.0?

No pun intended. (Last one, I promise!)

"Hey, Cecily," Marcus says, walking over to her. "What happened? I thought you were going to meet me here and watch us play?"

"I know, I'm really sorry," she replies. "Tryouts ran late and because I made the squad, I had to go out with the new girls afterward—it's like a whole tradition thing. I heard your last song; it was great!"

"Thanks. Congratulations, I guess. Hopefully next time you'll be able to hear the whole set. I think it was a pretty tight show."

"Trey said you were awesome. So . . . do you still want to hang out now?"

"Uhm, sure. Let me just put my gear away."

When I'm done eavesdropping on Cecily and Marcus's conversation, I look down next to me only to notice that Colin, who was holding my hand not three minutes ago, is suddenly over by the counter talking to Black Mop Head. I look up at the stage and Miles is still sitting there packing up his things. I decide to go show him the pictures I took.

I walk over to Colin and Georgia and interrupt them, rudely, asking for the camera. He gives it to me without question, and I march over to the stage, hoping that Colin's eyes are still on me.

I climb up the steps and walk over to where Miles is sitting.

"Hey, great set tonight," I say.

"Thanks. I'm Miles, I don't think we've met."

"I'm Lucy. I'm kind of new here."

"So I've heard. You seem to be making quite an impression in your short afterlife."

"Uh-oh, should I be afraid?"

"Nah, all good things," he says, and offers up another smile.

"Well, I wanted to show you these pictures I took. I think you're gonna like them."

He looks at me kind of funny, so I hand him the camera and let him flip through it to see for himself.

"Wow! These are unbelievable! It's been a really long time since I've seen myself in a picture. You must be pretty talented."

"You're pretty, too. I mean you're pretty *talented*, too, you're talented . . . you know, with the music . . . is what I meant to say. On the keyboard and singing and stuff."

Stop talking, Lucy, please stop talking!

"Right."

Before I can say anything else embarrassing, I decide to call it a night.

"Okay, well, I'm gonna go now," I say, taking back Colin's camera. "Maybe I'll see you around."

"Maybe you will."

I come back down from the stage and Cecily, Marcus, Colin, and Georgia are the only ones still here.

"We're gonna go to the arcade for a bit," Colin tells me. "Ready?"

I want to ask him to define "we" but I don't need to. Georgia is standing right there, staring at me, and the person I used to be able to count on to help ice Georgia out is now the newest member of her entourage.

"Actually I'm just going to go home. Here's your camera."

"Are you sure?" he says, pulling me aside. "If Georgia's the reason you don't want to come, just don't let her bother you, please?"

"Yeah . . . the thing is, what you *should* be saying right now is that if Georgia's the problem, you'll just tell her *she's* not invited—especially since she doesn't seem to have any trouble not inviting me places."

He says nothing, and I've been crushed enough for one day.

It's getting awfully tight in this compactor.

THE
LIMBO CENTRAL
CLUB MANUAL

RULE #5:

Every club has a faculty advisor. This
advisor must commit to overseeing the club
and helping it attain its goals. If you are
searching for a faculty advisor, it would
behoove you to find someone with some
experience in your chosen field.

Chapter Six
Brrr, It's Cold in Here

It's been two days since everything went down at the Clairvoyance Café, but it feels more like half a century. I literally could not be any happier that it's Friday.

Cecily and I are in the midst of what you could call a cold war. We're not completely ignoring each other, but, boy, is it icy. Does it suck? Totally. But I refuse to back down. As far as I'm concerned, she's playing right into Georgia's hands. If she wants to choose Cheerleading and Georgia over Dance Club and her best friend, well, she's just going to have to lady up and tell me to my face. I mean, yes, she did go out to the Spooky Soda Shoppe with them, which apparently is a "tradition" or whatever. But that doesn't definitively mean that she's decided to join the squad. Does it?

Or does it.

In the meantime, I have my own work to do for the Limbos, which I've been completely neglecting. I still need to get four people to sign up for the club—assuming Cecily is a no-go—and find a faculty advisor who has experience with this kind of thing. Maybe Ms. Keaner knows if any of the teachers used to dance, like, back in the day? I decide to go hit her up for answers before lunch. I want to ask her for the list of acts from the Winter Wonderland talent show, anyway, like Mia suggested. And it's not as if I'm itching to go to lunch and sit in awkward silence with Cecily, Georgia, and Colin right now.

Not a chance.

The bell rings, and it's time to go to my first-period class. When I close my locker door, Colin is standing behind it.

"Truce?" he says, holding out his hand to shake mine. He's smiling again and his dimple is showing, so I'm pretty sure he's trying to be flirty.

So not working.

"A truce suggests that we're fighting," I say, walking in the direction of my first class, Beginner's Telekinesis. "I'm not fighting with you. I just don't like the way you treated me."

Colin follows me.

"Okay, in all seriousness, I'm sorry. I guess I still get kind of tangled up in Georgia's stuff sometimes. I'm so used to saying yes to her that I forget, you know, to say no, or whatever."

"So I'm supposed to just accept that you're wired to let Georgia's needs come first, and do whatever she wants?"

"No, that's not what I mean. I just mean . . . it's hard to stop, like, a habit."

"Yeah, well, habits are a lot harder to break when you don't know if you really want to break them."

"What does that mean?"

Brrrrring! Brrrrring! Second first-period bell.

"You should go. You're going to be late," I tell him, walking into my class.

The rest of the morning scrolls by in blurry slow motion, like an old movie. When the lunch bell finally rings I head straight to Ms. Keaner's office.

"Oh, hello, Lucy!" she says, noticing me right away. "How are you?"

"I'm okay," I reply. "Do you have a minute?"

"Of course! As a matter of fact I was just going to summon you. How fortuitous! I have something I want to discuss with you."

"Really? What is it?"

"You first, dear! Come on into my office and tell me, what's on your mind?"

We enter her office and I sit down. It's a weird feeling. The last time I was in here was my very first day in Limbo. I couldn't even sit, and I kept falling through the chairs.

Flashback Friday.

(That's a thing, right?)

"Well, I'm thinking of starting a new club. A Dance Club called the Limbos."

"I see," she says, thoughtfully. "That sounds like a lovely idea. Is this something you and Cecily will be doing together? Because, you know, it's very hard work to start a club from scratch—especially as a new ghost who's still getting her bearings. It would be ideal for you to have a partner to help you out, and I know you two used to dance together."

"Uhm, I don't know," I say, honestly. "I thought Cecily was going to be a part of it, at first, but now she's thinking of joining the Cheerleading Squad."

"Ah, yes, that is a popular one. Not many girls get chosen. Georgia joins the ranks this year of the many fiercely dedicated and demanding captains who came before her."

I can only muster a half smile.

"I trust you know about the rules you'll need to follow to officially submit your club?"

"Yes, which is why I'm here," I reply, getting back on track. "I need members, and I was hoping you had the list of acts from the Winter Wonderland talent show last year? Mia Bennett told me that there were a few dance acts in the show. I'd like to approach those students to see if they have any interest."

"Well, aren't you two clever! Yes, I believe I have it right here in this folder."

She reaches into her file cabinet and pulls out a purple folder with flowers on it from the back of the drawer. She looks down the list of acts and gives me five names.

"Was there anything else you wanted to ask me?" she says, sweetly.

"Actually, yes. Do you know if any of the faculty members here have dance experience? You know, to advise the club."

"As a matter of fact, it just so happens that Ms. Tilly has quite an extensive background in dance. She was a professional ballroom dancer, you know, in her past life."

"Ms. Tilly as in Principal Tilly?"

"Yes, dear."

"Would she even have time to advise a club? I mean, is that, like, allowed?"

"You'll just have to ask her yourself, won't you?" she replies with a smirk.

I move to get up, but she places her hand on my arm to stop me.

"Before you go, there is something I wanted to talk to you about as well."

"Oh right, yes. What's that?" I say, sitting back down.

"As you know, news travels fast around here, and it has come to my attention that you are quite the talented photographer. It takes a very special kind of ghost to be able to perform this craft well—it's one of the trickiest and most temperamental art forms for us. I suppose I knew from the moment I met you that you had a most particular type of energy."

"Well, thank you," I whisper, humbly.

"Anyway, the Limbo Central Museum of Contemporary Art hosts an amateur night every fall, and I think you should submit your photographs. It is a competition, but anyone who wants to participate can. The winner gets a room in the museum all to themselves to exhibit their work for a whole month! Isn't that exciting?"

"Very," I say, stunned. "I'm so honored that you thought of me for this. Thank you."

"Those photographs of Miles Rennert really speak for themselves, don't they?"

I must look confused (mainly since I am), because she goes on to say this:

"You see, I'm afraid I can't take the credit for this idea. Colin Reed showed the photos to me and suggested you might be a good fit for this. He participated last year."

"Oh. So . . . when is it?"

"Ah yes, see dear, that's the only—what do they call it? Catch. The show is right around the corner—it's next Saturday on October thirty-first. They like to have fun, you know, with it being Halloween and all. That is when all the ghosts come out!"

She chuckles lightly to herself, and I can't help but laugh a little, too. Then she continues, "The entry deadline is today, so you will need to decide by the end of the day."

"I'll do it!" I say, triumphantly.

This could not be more perfect. October 31—Halloween night—the night of Georgia's stupid ghostday bash that I'm not invited to? Now instead of sitting home alone when all of my so-called friends are at her party, I'll be rubbing elbows with Limbo Central's elite artsy crew! There's nothing like being with super cool, creative people to take your mind off of not being invited to the biggest party of the year. Right?

"Excellent!" Ms. Keaner says. "I'll call the committee and alert them right now. Take these forms and fill them out, and drop them back here before the end of the day."

"Thanks, Ms. Keaner!"

"You're very welcome, Lucy."

I decide to skip lunch altogether and go see if Ms. Tilly is in her office. If she's not game to advise the Limbos, I'm going to need another plan. I walk into her office and tell the secretary I'd like a few minutes with the principal. While I wait, I start to get nervous. What if she asks me all kinds of questions about the club that I can't answer? The official club petition form asks you to state a purpose for the club, why it's important, and how it will incorporate ghost skills. I know that last part already, but what about why it's important? I think back to when Cecily and I were dancing and try to remember all the reasons we did it. Why was it so empowering? Why did we work so hard and practice so much?

"Ms. Chadwick?" the secretary calls out. "Ms. Tilly will see you now."

I enter her office, and my nerves kick into high gear. I mean, this is the PRINCIPAL! What was I thinking? Do I want this club so badly that I'm willing to throw myself to the sharks?! What person in her right mind knowingly—

voluntarily—marches into the principal's office and asks to spend MORE time with her?

It's B.A.N.A.N.A.S.

"Ms. Chadwick," Ms. Tilly says as I open the door, "please, come in."

"Thanks."

"What can I do for you?"

"Well, uhm, I'm sort of thinking of starting a new club."

"Really? That's ambitious for a new student. What kind of club?"

"Uhm, it's a dance club. It's going to be like ballet mixed with contemporary routines set to popular music. We're going to stage it with backdrops and do the costumes and everything. We're going to be called the Limbos."

Ms. Tilly flashes me a big smile and then attempts to cover it up ever so slightly, almost as if her own reaction took her by surprise.

"That *is* ambitious," she concludes. "I like the name very much."

"Thanks."

"So, what brings you to me, then? How can I possibly help you in your endeavor?"

"You can be my club's faculty advisor."

From the look of her shocked expression, no one's ever asked her this before. That's probably because no student is half as crazy as I am. And make no mistake, at this moment? I am.

Crazy.

After a few seconds, she still seems stunned. So I go on.

"See, I heard that you used to be a pretty serious dancer. A professional. You know, back when you were alive. And I really need someone who understands what being a dancer is all about."

"And . . . what is being a dancer all about to you?" she asks, thoughtfully.

"It's about discipline, self-expression, and hard work. But it's also about being part of a community, you know? I was a ballet dancer, you know, *before*, and even though I felt like I was part of a group, I didn't always feel like we had each other's backs. So I want this club to be better than that. And . . . it's a great way to feel connected to another person. When you share a love of dance with someone, it's, like, completely different from anything else. I don't know how to describe it . . . but it's really overpowering."

I finish talking and more silence ensues. I think about Cecily. How much fun we would have had doing this together.

How important dance used to be to her—how we shared that so completely. It's what bonded us together. And if that goes away, what happens to us?

"That's very insightful," Ms. Tilly finally replies.

"Thanks," I say quietly.

More silence.

I feel like I'm awaiting some kind of sentencing, like when I did something wrong and my parents were deciding how to punish me. It's really nerve-racking! I start to doubt my decision to come in here. What if this was the worst idea EVER? What if she's not only going to say no? What if she's going to tell me that I'm not ready to start a club on my own or I'm not doing it for the right reasons and she makes me drop the whole idea completely?

Calm down, Lucy, this is not the end of the world. Take some deep breaths before your emotions attack THE PRINCIPAL.

"My answer is yes."

"Yes!" I shout, jumping out of my chair. "Yes, like yes? You'll do it?"

"Yes, that's what yes means."

"I can't believe it. I thought for sure you were going to say no."

"Nope," she says, cheerily. "And in fact, I'm honored that you even asked me. I've never been asked to advise a club before. I think most students are scared of me."

"Psh, scared? That's silly!"

I must be having some sort of fit to be talking to my principal this way, but who cares. SHE SAID YES!!!!!!

"Okay, we'll discuss details another time. Run along now—the fifth-period bell is going to ring soon."

"Yes, of course. Thank you!" I cry, halfway out of her office.

When I walked into school this morning, things were looking mighty drab. But now? I have to admit they are starting to turn. I have my handy list of people to scout out for the Limbos, I have the coolest, most powerful faculty advisor of all time, AND I'm enrolled in the amateur art night at the museum, which is WAY better than some stupid old ghostday party being thrown by someone I can't stand.

Just then the bell rings, and everyone exits the cafeteria. I notice the herd of cheerleaders, all still dressed in their uniforms even though tryouts are officially O.V.E.R. Not that I'm surprised. Georgia will do whatever it takes to get them to follow her around for the rest of her life.

I spot Colin and switch gears. "Colin!" I call out.

He sees me and comes over.

"I just wanted to thank you for suggesting that art contest to Ms. Keaner," I tell him. "I'm going to do it."

"That's great," he says. "Your photos are really good."

"Thanks," I say. "Well, you thinking about me means a lot."

He smiles. "My buddy who volunteers for the show said they were still looking for submissions—so it seems like fate."

"Right."

At that exact moment the cheerleaders parade by us, and I see Cecily in her shiny new uniform. Well, it's not the exact uniform. She isn't powerful enough to make the whole thing, so she just changed the colors of her existing outfit to gray-and-white. But she did manage to change the tutu into a regular skirt a couple of days ago.

Colin sees her walking toward me and he takes off to class, leaving us alone.

"So, I guess you're officially part of the cheerleading squad now," I say.

"I guess I am," she replies.

"And you didn't feel like you owed it to me to at least be up front and tell me that—I mean, before you started gallivanting around the school in uniform?"

"I don't know," she says, kind of coolly. "It sort of feels like I always owe you something these days, and this time, I just wanted to make a decision and do something that I wanted to do without having to get your permission first."

"Wow, Georgia is already rubbing off on you, isn't she?"

"You're one to talk!" she shouts, angrily. "Isn't it just like Georgia to make your friends feel bad for having opinions and desires that are different from yours? Isn't it just like Georgia to make your friends choose between things and people? How about being so wrapped up in your own afterlife and what you want that you don't even listen to what your friends want? That sounds an awful lot like Georgia to me."

My jaw drops open. "I can't believe you just said that."

"Well, I can't believe you said it first."

The second bell rings and everyone in the hallway disperses, quickly. Cecily is the first to break our gaze. She turns on her heels and heads off to class.

So much for telling her my big news.

Or for finishing conversations. Apparently.

This cold war? Just froze over.

You have an incoming Tabulator message!

Ms. Lucy Chadwick
Congratulations on submitting
your work to the Limbo Central Museum
of Contemporary Art's Annual
Amateur Exhibit!
You are among a small and elite
group of young talented artists, and
you should be very proud of what
you have accomplished.
Contestants are asked to show
up at the museum by 4 p.m. on Saturday
to arrange their work.
50 Harbor Avenue
The reception* begins at 7 p.m.
Food and drinks will be served.
Awards will be announced at 9 p.m.
—The LCMOCA Board
*Please feel free to invite whomever
would like to come support you.
This event is free and open
to the Limbo public.

Chapter Seven
She Said, She Said

It's Saturday morning and I need to get out of this room and far away from the roommate who's been ignoring me since yesterday.

Like, get out *now*.

I've been trying to thaw out from our nasty post-lunch exchange since it happened, but nothing seems to be working. Usually when we fight it only takes about an hour, sometimes even less, for both of us to come around and see the other person's point of view. Before we know it, we're apologizing, hugging it out, and eating chocolate-chip cookie dough ice cream (the *only* acceptable flavor) out of the carton while we binge-watch our favorite show, *It's Not You, It's Me*, which is about two classmates who have a *Freaky Friday* moment and swap bodies. But this fight feels different. I'm not second-guessing myself or wondering how she's feeling, or even feeling bad about the things that I said. The only thing I've got going on right now is a supersize portion of anger.

I kind of just want to disappear for a bit and get away from all the drama, so I meet up with Mia and she's taking me somewhere around Limbo that I haven't been yet. We get on a bus and head up to the mountains where the ski lodge is. One of the coolest things about being able to control energy is that you can control the climate, too. So Limbo isn't stuck with just one; we can have the beach and the snow, like, almost next to each other.

The only good thing that's happened in the last twenty-four hours? Word that Ms. Tilly is going to be my faculty advisor made its way around school so quickly yesterday that some girl in my last period Ghost Hunters class actually told *me* about it—not knowing I'm, well, me.

Insanity.

Apparently everyone here really likes Ms. Tilly—or they think that having her in charge of the Limbos will evoke some special treatment for its members—because before the day ended on Friday I got about ten people to sign up! Now I can officially submit my forms and petition list and all that jazz.

Pun intended! (Get it?)

Finally things are starting to fall into place.

Well, not *all* things. Okay, not even most things.

Fine! One thing. One thing is in place.

Still, a thing's a thing, right?

"Sometimes, when I'm feeling meh," Mia says, snapping me out of my internal dialogue, "I come up here and ride the lifts for hours. It's peaceful, you know? And seeing how big the world is really helps put things into perspective. For me, anyway."

"Sounds great. I'll take any perspective I can get right about now. And any chance to relax and calm down. I'm just so . . . mad."

We step up to the loading area, and the lift guy opens the door of the cable car for us to slide in. He shuts it, makes sure it's locked, and we start moving. The view from up here is spectacular. Frosted white peaks against a backdrop of grayish-lavender sky, and when I look back toward the direction we came from I can still see blue water and white, sandy beach. Even California isn't this beautiful.

We get about halfway across the long trip to the highest peak in silence, and then Mia says this:

"Did I ever tell you that Georgia and I used to be, like, really good friends?"

"What?" I belt out, shocked.

"Yeah. When I first got to Limbo, she was my tutor. And we actually got along really well. She wasn't my usual type of friend, you know, but we clicked. Also, she wasn't quite as popular as she is now, but she did have a lot of friends. Or people who wanted to be her friend. But I think at the time she was kind of, I don't know, searching for something real— something she wasn't finding with other people—because she seemed to really open up to me."

"Okay . . ."

"She told me stuff about her life, like, before she crossed over. She was adopted so that has a lot to do with why she wants to be so popular and have so many friends. Anyway, I don't want to air all of her private stuff, but she had a difficult life before Limbo."

"Why are you telling me this?" I ask, a little taken aback.

"I guess because everyone comes from somewhere; everyone is more than what we see, you know, on the outside. And because I think you should know."

"Okay, so is that it?"

"No. We became pretty close—this was before she was friends with Chloe—and after a few months we had even decided that the next year we wanted to live together. Georgia told me I was the first person in her life—or afterlife—who she felt like she could really trust. It was a pretty big deal. It all happened quickly. I mean, I think I was only in Limbo about five months before things started to go sour. That's when Trey started to like me. And Georgia got jealous."

"Of course she did! Because all the boys have to like *her*, don't they?"

"Actually she wasn't jealous of me, she was jealous of Trey."

"What?"

"Here, she had made her first real friend ever, and in comes this guy trying to take my time away from her. She was jealous of Trey because now she had to share me. I know this story makes me sound like a total egomaniac and that's so not true. It's just, that's what happened. One day she picked a really big fight with me and told me that I had to choose between her and him. I told her that was completely unfair, and that I had room for both of them in my afterlife. But I think she expected me to immediately choose her, and she was really hurt when I didn't. After that fight, she basically broke up with me. She stopped talking to me, wouldn't answer any of my Holomails or calls. I told her I was sorry and that I wanted to make it up to her, that I still really wanted to be her friend and I would make more of an effort to make time for her, but nothing worked. It was like I had lost her trust, and that was that."

The cable car pulls up to the top of the mountain, and the door opens automatically. Technically we're supposed to jump out and ski down the mountain, but neither of us gets up. We didn't plan on skiing. We let the door close again and the car turns around and heads back the way we came.

"Are you seriously telling me that you miss being friends with Georgia?" I ask, incredulously.

"Yes and no. The Georgia you know, the Georgia that exists today, is not the same Georgia who I was friends with. Or maybe she is, but she's just got more protective layering. Georgia does the things Georgia does because she's scared of getting hurt and letting people see that. When we were friends, she trusted me enough to open up and then I really hurt her. And now she's not taking any chances."

"So, are you saying that you're the reason why Georgia is so awful?"

"I don't know. I mean, yes, I hurt her, but I also apologized and it was her choice not to forgive me. So, that's on her, you know? I'm not about to take the blame for how she behaves or reacts to things."

"Okay . . . that's fair. But are you saying that you regret choosing Trey over her?"

"No, I don't."

"I'm confused."

"Look, I think what Georgia did to me was wrong. She never should have made me choose between her and Trey. It wasn't fair. And it just goes to show you how awful ultimatums can be . . . making someone choose between people never ends well. But, just because what she did was unfair doesn't mean I like the way things turned out."

"Oh . . . so you think *I'm* making Cecily choose between me and Georgia? Because I'm not. Georgia is making her choose, just like she did with you."

"But . . . you kind of are," Mia replies. "I mean, yes, Georgia made up that stupid club rule, but you're making it seem like Cecily choosing Cheerleading over Dance Club is like Cecily choosing Georgia over you. And it's not."

"It kind of sounds like you're on Georgia's side," I say, frustrated. I thought this was going to be calming, and it's turning out to be anything but.

"I'm not! I'm on your side—and I don't think you're going to win like this. People aren't black and white. Georgia isn't all evil and no good. I'm not saying I, like, approve of the things she does. All I'm saying is there's always a reason why she does them, you just have to look for it. It's just easier to act like a Georgia than we all think, because Georgia's not just some mean girl. She's real, and she gets hurt, and she gets scared. Just like you're hurt and scared you're going to lose Cecily . . . so you're trying to force her to do this Dance Club thing when you know she really wants to do Cheerleading instead."

"I . . . I'm not . . . I just . . . What if . . . Aw, man."

UGH.

"There it is!" she says, all smiles.

"Did you just bring me on this thing so you could hold me hostage until I agree with you?" I ask, half joking.

"Basically," she says. "Works every time."

Sunday rolls around and I still haven't seen Cecily. She's, like, disappeared, or something. I decide to head to Colin's to borrow his camera for the day. The art show is only a week away, and I need to decide what photographs I want to display. Some of the ones I took of Miles were pretty interesting, but I don't want to limit myself to just photos of him. I mean, if I do that I'll totally look like I'm into him.

No, thank you!

I get to Dickens House and buzz Colin's room. The door clicks, letting me know he's opened it, and his hologram appears.

"Hey," he says. "We're in the game room on three."

I'm really hoping "we" means him and Marcus. It took me all night to Zen out about the Georgia/Cecily situation, but if I get upstairs and see them all here together my Zen attitude will last for about two-and-a-half minutes max before going belly-up.

I get there and walk in on what looks to me like yet another double date. Only this time, it's not mine.

Can I get two minutes and thirty seconds on the clock, please?

02:30

(Thank you.)

Cecily and Marcus are playing virtual chess, and it looks like Colin and Georgia were in the middle of finishing their zombie video game when he paused it to come get me.

02:20.

"Oh, hey," Cecily says, utterly surprised.

"What's *she* doing here?" Georgia whispers to Colin, who sits back down next to her and picks up his controller. He rolls his eyes but says nothing.

02:12.

"*She* came to see if Colin would lend her his camera," I answer, loudly.

"What for? It's such a dumb pastime," Georgia says, all holier-than-thou.

Just then Colin gets up and leaves, I assume to go get me his camera.

Georgia gets distracted by Colin's exit for a moment but then decides to keep talking. "I mean, no one ever shows up in them. What's the point of taking pictures if you can't, like, capture the beauty of people?"

"Not all people are beautiful," I reply.

01:42

"Duh," Marcus says. "Where have you been all week? Lucy's, like, super gifted. Everyone she takes pictures of shows up. It's all over the school."

Georgia's snooty expression fades, and suddenly she looks like one of the evil stepsisters whose foot doesn't fit the slipper.

HA.

01:31

"So you can, like, take actual pictures," Georgia directs at me in a tone that's half normal. "Like, with people in them?"

"Not that it makes a difference to you, but yes," I say, trying to be civil.

I keep looking over at Cecily, who's pretending to study the chessboard every time I look at her. I'm trying to keep in mind what Mia said yesterday, but it's taking all my energy to not scream at both of them right now.

"Cool," Georgia says. Her tone seems to be getting friendlier and I'm starting to wonder what she's got up her sleeve when she hands it to me. "So, you're coming to my ghostday party on Saturday night, aren't you?"

Everyone in the room turns to look at her like she just ate glue.

01:01

"Why would I be coming to a party I wasn't invited to?" I ask, nonchalantly.

"Of course you were invited, silly!" she says, dramatically. "The invite must have just gotten lost or spammed or something. You *have* to come. And you should bring Colin's camera and take pictures of everyone! I'll give you the VIP inside scoop all night long."

I can't help but burst out laughing. Is this girl for real?

00:50

Just then Colin comes back with his camera in tow and hands it to me. "Here you go. What'd I miss?"

"Just Georgia being incredibly self-serving, as usual. Georgia, as much as I'd *love* to come to your party that you didn't invite me to until you realized you could use me, and I mean that sarcastically, in case that wasn't clear, I have something very important to do that night. I'll be showing my photos at the Limbo Central Museum of Contemporary Art Annual Amateur Exhibit that night. It's going to be very cool, lots of elite, artistic folks. Free food, drinks, the works. You guys should all come! It's open to the public. Except, not you, obviously, Georgia. You're having your party, and all."

00:27

I look over at Cecily, and she has her sad puppy-dog face on. I didn't mean to tell her like this, I just couldn't resist stinging Georgia back.

And Georgia does look stung. She's wondering if any of her friends are going to choose my thing over her thing now. But I don't care how sad and hurt she is on the inside; she can't keep treating people like this. There are consequences to her actions. Besides, it's not like I invited them out of spite. I would have told them about it eventually. It's up to them where they want to spend the night, I'm just giving them options. They're my friends, too. I think.

"Very cool," Marcus says, breaking through the silence and death glares. (Hee-hee.) "You're definitely going to win."

"Well, I don't know about that, but I'm excited to be a part of it," I tell him. "It's all thanks to Colin. He's the one who told Ms. Keaner about my photos."

00:09

"Actually I should probably get going," I say. Whatever Zen I have left in me is fading fast, and even if it wasn't? I'm so ready to leave this place. "Got a lot of pictures to take today."

Then Cecily finally speaks. "Maybe we can stop by before Georgia's party on Saturday?"

"Sure," I say, lifting up the camera and zooming in tight on Georgia's crushed face.

00:03

00:02

00:01

Click.

LIMBO CENTRAL
MIDDLE SCHOOL

Limbo Central's newest club is officially
here! The Limbos is Limbo Central's
new Dance Club.
Do you like to dance?
Do you love being creative and working
with other creative people?
DO YOU LOVE TO HAVE FUN?!
Pop. Contemporary. Hip-hop.
You name it—we'll be doing it!
Come to the auditorium on Tuesday
at 4 p.m. for our first meeting.
If you show up, you're in the Limbos!
It's as simple as that.

Your Limbos Dance Captain,
Lucy Chadwick

Chapter Eight
Limbo Fever

I've officially submitted all of my forms for the Limbos!

At last.

And with Ms. Tilly as my advisor? I'm not sweating getting approval even a little bit. What I am sweating? Is our first meeting today at 4 P.M. in the auditorium.

Also, it's Tuesday, which means my first two periods are Paranormal Energy, with Cecily, and we're lab partners. Things between us are still super awkward. After Sunday, when she mentioned coming to my show, I thought things would change. But they haven't. I mean, we're not completely ignoring each other anymore and we don't seem to be quite as angry—at least I'm not. But things haven't gone back to normal. This morning she left for school before I even woke up!

I hate this. I'm so over fighting. And I can't lie; my conversation with Mia was actually pretty helpful, after I stopped being so irritated by it. It's not like I'm suddenly interested in being BFFs with Georgia and forgiving her for all the rotten things she does, but I see Mia's point. It's a lot easier to be a Georgia than I thought it was. I was kind of being Georgia myself, earlier.

GASP.

And I think I know why. But so was Cecily!

Ugh. I just wish we could talk about it!!!

BAM! My locker door slams shut on its own, thanks to my uncontrollable angry energy.

Hola, Emotional Girl, welcome back!

"Whoa, be careful! You could kill someone with that," Cecily jokes.

"Oh, jeez, sorry!" I say, surprised.

"Well, thankfully I'm already dead, so no harm done."

She's trying to be funny, which is weird on a regular day let alone Day Four of the worst fight we've ever had.

"Right," I say, nervously. "Well, we should get to class."

"I'm excited about your show," she says, as we walk together.

"You are?"

"Yeah! I think it's great."

"You do?"

"Why wouldn't I?"

"I don't know."

"What time does it start?"

"Seven, and the award ceremony is at nine."

"Cool. So we'll plan to come to you first and hang out until the ceremony's over, then head over to Georgia's. I just need to make an appearance. You know, for the squad."

This is the most we've spoken in a week, and even though I'm happy about it, I have questions.

"What's going on?" I ask, matter-of-factly.

"Nothing really. I'm just happy about the show and I want to come see it."

"That's great, but I mean, why are you suddenly talking to me and willing to miss Georgia's party to see my show when we haven't even spoken in, like, four days? And you're not even saying anything about the fight—you're just acting like things have been totally normal?"

"I guess because we've never really fought like this before and I don't know how to behave. Everything feels weird."

"That's fair," I say. "But we really need to talk about what happened."

The first bell rings, and everyone in the hallway starts to disperse toward their first-period classes.

"Look," she begins. "It's hard always being second best to your best friend."

"What do you mean?" I screech, getting heated. "You're never second best to me!"

"Hold up, that's not what I mean. What I mean is that to everyone else, you're always the best, and I'm always second. Or third. Or fourth. You're the better dancer. You're the more powerful ghost, who changed her clothes in, like, record speed. You're the more talented ghost, who can take these amazing photos—something ghosts who've been around for years can't even do. I just got tired of always being 'Lucy's friend.' This time I wanted to be known on my own, to do something different and be good at it without being compared to you. And I knew you would never do cheerleading. And it is something I like to do."

"I had no idea that's how you were feeling," I say, because I didn't. Suddenly everything feels totally different. I feel so silly.

The second bell rings and Mr. Orville tells us to settle down. I try to whisper back to Cecily when he's not paying attention. Every time he looks at me I freeze.

"I'm sorry," I say quietly. "I never meant for you to feel that way."

"Did someone say something?" Mr. Orville says, turning around.

No one speaks, so he turns back to the board and continues to write up the lab instructions.

"I wish you had told me," I whisper. "I just . . . I thought I was losing you to her. I thought if we didn't do Dance Club together, maybe we'd lose what we have in common the most. And maybe we wouldn't stay friends."

"Okay, I know I heard something that time!" he warns. "It's not time to talk; it's time to listen."

The class laughs quietly.

Cecily takes out a piece of paper and scribbles something down, then hands it to me when he's not looking again.

> You will never lose me. Dancing may be the reason we became friends, but it's not the reason we became <u>best</u> friends. But friends need to let friends branch out and try new things. Deal?
>
> -Cece

Deal. As long as joining the Cheerleading Squad doesn't mean you're going to be friends with Georgia and play into her mean behavior. I still need you to have my back with her. Even if that means your captain is going to be mad at you. Some things are personal. Deal?

-Lou

Deal. For the record I wasn't siding with her, I was just mad at you. It has to be okay for me to want to do things with her without it seeming like I'm turning into her. Or choosing her over you. Like, I really wanted to go to the Spooky Soda Shoppe after tryouts. It was a tradition. I know you thought it was stupid, or whatever, and that's fine. But you shouldn't make me feel bad about it. Sometimes we have to make tough decisions, and we can't always do what other people want us to do. But it doesn't mean we're being Georgias.

-Cece

It's not that you went, it's that you didn't seem to care that you were hurting people's feelings. With Marcus and with me. You should have told me you didn't want to do Dance Club. You should have been honest instead of letting me see you parade around the school in uniform. It really hurt my feelings.

-Lou

Cecily opens the note, writes something, then folds it up again to hand it back to me.

I reach out to grab it when Mr. Orville turns around for the first time in fifteen minutes.

"What is *that*?" he calls out, staring at the note that is now floating in the air squarely between my desk and Cece's.

Uh-oh.

"Are you girls passing notes in my class?" he says, and neither of us says a thing. "Hand it over, now."

It's clear he means business, and I start panicking. I lose my concentration, and the note—the same piece of paper we've been vomiting our feelings all over for the last twenty minutes—falls to the floor.

"Okay, then, I'll just get it myself," he says, willing the

note to float over to him. "Whatever you're writing about must be much more interesting than what I'm trying to teach you," Mr. Orville continues. "Perhaps we should just read the note aloud to the class and let them decide?"

Okay, first of all, the obvious answer to that is what we're writing is WAY more interesting.

Second? I despise this teacher tactic. It's a completely unequal punishment for the crime. What he's been writing on the board is obviously not private—I mean, it's on the board!

DUH.

The fact that we have to pass notes signifies that whatever we're writing about can't be said out loud. Embarrassing us by reading our innermost thoughts and feelings in front of other students is just plain cruel.

I'm so annoyed right now I could scream! Cecily and I were having a serious conversation in that letter. We've been fighting for four days! Four days! We needed to vent.

"AHHHH!" Mr. Orville screams suddenly, and I'm yanked out of my melodramatic inner freak-out session. "Fire! Fire!"

The note. Is on. FIRE.

I literally made the note go up in flames. IN HIS HANDS!!

No one knows what to do. Under normal, non-afterlife circumstances, we would all be rushed to the nearest exit and counted off like sheep. But since this is the Spirit World and everything, we all just sit here awaiting further instruction. Or ignoring it altogether. I mean, I'm pretty sure fire isn't all that deadly to ghosts.

Ha.

Cecily looks at me and mouths, "I'm sorry."

I smile back at her. "Me too."

Mr. Orville puts the fire out, and everything goes back to normal.

Finally.

School is out and the Limbos first meeting is happening in, like, three minutes. Cecily doesn't have cheer practice today, so she's coming to watch! It's such a relief to have the Cecily fight over with. I feel like a totally new ghost.

But, like, in a good way.

I look down the list of twelve people who signed up, and I'm surprised to see Miles and Oliver Rennert on the list. I didn't notice those names the last time I checked.

This can't be right.

"Uh, Cecily, is this who I think it is?"

"Miles and Oliver Rennert," she reads. "Yup, I think it is. Miles has a younger brother named Oliver, I'm pretty sure."

"Miles can't be a dancer. It's like, just, impossible."

"Well, I think you're about to find out exactly how possible it is."

It's four on the dot, and people start filing into the gym. Sure enough, there's Miles and a kid who I assume is Oliver walking next to him. Miles makes his way over to me.

"Hey, stranger," he says.

"Hey yourself," I reply. Okay, I'm not even trying to be cutesy, but my words sound SUPER flirty. How does THAT happen?! "So, what brings you to the Limbos?"

"Moral support?" he says. "My little brother is an awesome dancer, but he has this feeling he's going to be the only guy—so I decided to come with him and see what's up."

Uh, hello, is he kidding right now? Could he be any sweeter?

"Wow, that's very big brother-y and protective of you," I say.

Just then Ms. Tilly appears by my side, and it's time to get started.

"Okay, thank you all for being here!" I say, enthusiastically.

"I'm really excited to have our first official Limbos meeting. As you probably know, Ms. Tilly is here to advise us. She used to be a professional ballroom dancer! Which is super cool, and means we're in excellent hands. My whole reason for starting this club is that I love to dance, and I think it's a great way to have fun while learning the value of hard work, and it's also a great way to make friends and feel like you're part of a community. So, I want us all to feel that way. That this club is our community. I'm the captain, but I'm going to do my best to listen to everyone and try to make everyone happy. We can decide where and what we perform, and what our costumes and sets are going to look like—everything—together, as a group. My goal is that we'll be able to perform at the Spring Fling Carnival at the end of the year. This is all brand-new to me, so please just remember that and cut me some slack if—*when*—I mess up. I'm totally open to suggestions. How does that sound?"

Everyone nods and smiles.

"Okay, great. So, let's sit in a circle and take some time to go around the room and get to know one another. Say your name, what year you're in, what kind of dance you like the best—or you're most comfortable with—and then tell us why you signed up and what you want the club to do."

It takes us about a half an hour to get all the way around the circle, and when we're done I put some music on and we do some freestyle dancing. People are allowed to do whatever they want, by themselves or in a group. It's awesome to see people collaborating on new things. Girls who don't even hang out during the school day are choreographing things together and having a blast being creative. Everyone is smiling.

Even Miles.

Except that he's not actually partaking in anything; he's just sitting on the side of the stage watching.

"What's this?" I say, sneaking up next to him. "Not participating?"

"Like I said, I'm only here for moral support. But if you need a mean break-dancer, I'm your guy."

"I'll keep that in mind," I say. Then I look over at Oliver, who's in a group with four other girls doing a jazz routine, spinning them each around like he's the king of the dance floor and they're his marionettes. "I think Oliver is gonna be just fine here. He seems to be fitting in swimmingly."

"Well, if *you* ever need to be lifted or thrown, just give me a call," he says with a smirk, then gets up to leave.

"Good to know."

Uhm, what just happened? Is *he* flirting with *me*? No, he can't be. I'm just hallucinating or something.

(Right?!)

"Lucy, come over here!" Oliver calls out. "We want to show you something!"

I go over to join him, and he introduces me to his group: Allie Kit, Lara Briar, Sasha Kats, and Ryan Hawking. "Come dance with us! We need a sixth."

For the rest of the time, I work on the routine with them. It was so freeing! And after the week I've had? I needed some serious release of pent-up energy. Also, Oliver is an insane dancer and a really strong partner, too.

This? Is gonna be amazing.

Before I know it, five thirty rolls around and it's time to go. I thank everyone for coming. "The meeting on Friday will be more organized, I promise!" I yell out as everyone heads to the locker rooms.

I'm gathering my stuff when I see Oliver walking toward me.

"So, my brother's into you," he says, smirking and swatting me playfully with his sweatshirt.

"Uhm, what?" I say, trying to act all nonchalant, but failing miserably.

Cecily joins us. "Hey, I'm Cecily," she says, holding out her hand for him to shake.

"Oliver," he says, shaking hers back. "So . . . Miles is into you. I know it, I can tell," he continues, all gossipy-like. "It's not like him to crush on someone so new and young, either . . ."

"Well that probably confirms the fact that he doesn't actually like me," I say.

"Uh, *excuse* me?" Oliver says, arguing with me. "Why do you think he showed up here today? It wasn't to put on pair of tights and leap across the gym like the rest of us."

"Wait, he said he came for moral support—because you were worried you'd be the only guy here."

"Oh, please! Does it look like I have any problem with who I am? Being the only guy in a sea of girlfriends is, like, my life. He came here for you."

"Miles Rennert is into Lou?" Cecily screeches.

"Shhh. . . ." I say, nervously.

She covers her mouth automatically. "I'm sorry," she whispers.

"Uhm, there's, like, nobody here but us," Oliver says. "And who's Lou?"

"I'm Lou."

"Wait, how do you know he's into her?" Cece asks Oliver, all excited.

"I just know. Miles is my brother—I'm very in tune with his M.O. He, like, could not stop talking about those pictures you took of him with the band that night. And Miles is a guy's guy, so he can pretty much stop talking about anything whenever he wants to."

"Oooh, this is getting good!" Cecily says. "But wait, what about Colin?"

"What about Colin?" I say. "I thought we were going to be something, but it's become pretty clear that we aren't. He can't seem to get over Georgia. She's, like, got him micro-chipped or something."

"Excuse my frankness," Oliver says, "but, girl, you can do so much better. I mean, Colin Reed is cute and all, but he's a child. Anyone who would date Georgia Sinclaire is in need of some serious growing up."

"I love you," I say jokingly to our new best friend.

"And why are you not in the Limbos?" Oliver reprimands Cecily, unprovoked. "I saw you in that ballet getup when you first got here. I *know* you can dance."

"Because I'm on Cheer Squad and Georgia won't let us do

more than one sports club. Says we need to be available and healthy to cheer for our Limbo teams."

"See? Total drama queen!" he says.

I burst out laughing.

"I didn't say a thing to him, I swear!" I tell Cece, but she starts laughing, too.

"Girls, we have our work cut out for us," Oliver says.

"You mean in the Limbos, or in the afterlife?" I ask, as if Oliver is some kind of oracle or psychic.

Just then Oliver's Tabby goes off. "Oops, I got to go," he says, heading toward the boys' locker room. "I'll see you on Friday! And wear more red—Miles loves red!"

"This was WAY more fun than cheer practice!" Cecily says, laughing. "And you really should wear more red."

What in the world just happened? Someone please pinch me to make sure I'm still alive?!

Oh, wait.

Never mind.

·THE
LIMBO CENTRAL
CLUB MANUAL

RULE #6:

Scheduling can be a problem at times, but
the faculty is more than happy to work
together to come up with a solution so
that students may be involved in as many
activities as they so choose.
Simply come to the administration
office and state your conflict, and we'll
do our best to fix the problem!

Chapter Nine
Team Lucily

"Let's go do something fun!" Cecily says, as we exit the school after Limbos practice.

"Like what?" I say. "It is a school night. We can't be out too late or we'll get in trouble."

"Who cares? We got the band back together! Team Lucily is back in full force. We have to celebrate."

"Wow, Cecily Vanderberg doesn't care if we get in trouble? Don't you, like, break out in hives if you even think a teacher is disappointed in you?"

"Funny. And yes. But tonight, it's a whole new me! I'm wild and free, baby."

"Hmmm . . . okay, well . . . Oh, I know! Let's go to the Ghostbuster's Theater and see a movie. We'll watch some horrible chick flick, get popcorn and candy, and totally do it up right."

"Sold!"

On our walk to Death Row, I take the opportunity to grill Cece about Marcus.

"So . . . what's going on with you two? How many times have you gone out?"

"Twice, but we haven't actually been alone on, like, a real date yet. We were *supposed* to on Sunday, but then Georgia basically inserted herself into our date when she found out I was going to see him. She just wanted a reason to tag along to see Colin—oh, I'm sorry."

"It's okay, really. So, you've seen him twice . . . and?"

"He's nice. And cute and sweet. He's the worst chess player ever. And he tells horrible jokes, but on purpose. Like, he knows they're bad, but does it anyway. I guess he's not afraid to look silly. And I like that."

"That's awesome—you seem to really like him."

"I think I do," she says, sweetly, staring off into space.

"So, how did you two leave things on Sunday?"

"Well, we finally got away from Georgia and Colin, and he walked me back to our dorm."

"And?"

"And . . . yes, okay, we kissed."

"Yippee!" I scream and clap, annoyingly.

"Don't get crazy, it was just one little, tiny kiss. But it was sweet. And he asked if I wanted to go with him to Georgia's party on Saturday night."

"That's cool," I say, unsure if this means she's changed her mind about my show.

"I told him that I really wanted to go to your show, and he said he didn't care where we went, as long as we were hanging out together."

"Awww . . . that's super cute!"

Cecily just smiles, but I wonder if she's holding something back to be nice. After everything with Colin, I think she feels bad for me and doesn't want to brag.

"You know how you said that it's hard always being second best to me?" I ask her.

She looks down at her hands, and then says, "Yeah."

"Well, you're not *always* second best. When it comes to this kind of thing—to boys and dating and stuff—you definitely come in first."

"Don't say that!" she says, all concerned.

"No, it's okay!" I reply, and it really is. "I'm not feeling bad about myself or anything. It's just the truth. You're better with guys. You're more sure of yourself, and you know how to do this whole dating thing. I'm awkward and emotional and I do weird things. And even things that I think are, like, sure things, get messed up. Like with Colin."

"I knew you were upset about that," she says.

"I'm not, not really. I mean, maybe I am a little bit. But it's more just me wondering what I did wrong, you know?"

"Oh my god, you didn't do anything wrong! He's a big dodo head."

"He's a *dodo head*?" I ask, smirking.

"Yes. That's what I said. And don't laugh at me!" she says, cracking up and fake swatting me on the arm.

"Okay," I say, smiling. "He's a dodo head."

"Well, he is. I mean, if Colin chooses Georgia over you, then he *really* isn't good enough for you. I don't care how cute he is. And if you don't believe me, you *have* to believe Oliver. We've only known him for what, like, two hours? And even *he* said that you can do way better than Colin!"

"I think he was just saying that to get me to like Miles."

"Uhm, who cares?! Miles is super cute and dreamy!"

We arrive at the theater and buy two tickets to the new romantic comedy *Cupcakes and Co.,* about a cupcake chef and the cute guy who lives above her shop. It's cheese at its absolute best—and I'm embarrassed I'm actually about to admit this but . . . I can't wait.

Rom-Com forever.

The only thing I'm slightly upset about? We don't have any cupcakes.

"I have been dying to see this movie!" Cecily squeals, excitedly.

"Okay, if I can predict what's going to happen, dinner's on you."

"I thought this *was* dinner," she says, nodding to our stash of M&M'S, Sno-Caps, Twizzlers, Sour Patch Kids, and medium-size popcorn.

"Not if *you're* buying! Okay, so . . . First they hate each other, but then they fall in love. Then they have a HUGE fight, but just when we think all is lost they make up and get married and live happily ever after."

"I did not agree to this bet," she says, all pouty.

"Ha! Because you know I'm right."

"Just watch the movie and try to be normal, please!"

Suddenly I spy a flash of straight black hair. I look over and sure enough, there's Georgia sitting next to Colin. I boost myself up on my knees to see into their laps, where his arm is lightly resting on her leg, and her hand is draped over his.

"Oh no," Cecily says, seeing what I see. "Are you okay? Do

you want to leave? Do you want to throw popcorn at the back of their heads?"

"Yes, no, and yes! Can we, pretty please, with popcorn on top?" I reply, smiling.

"I was just kidding about that one."

"Yeah, I knew you couldn't be that wild." I smirk back.

"So much for forgetting the outside world and just having fun together, huh?"

"Actually I think that was exactly what I needed to see. And I'm not going to let them ruin this amazing, soon-to-be critically acclaimed movie based on the literary masterpiece, *I'm Crying Cupcakes*!"

"Hilarious."

"I thought so," I reply, dropping a Sour Patch Kid into my mouth.

"There's the Lucy I know and love," she says, inhaling a handful of Sno-Caps.

At least somebody does.

Wednesday morning, Oliver comes up to my locker bright and early before the first-period bell rings.

"I just thought of the most brilliant idea!" he yells, excitedly.

"Good morning to you, too."

"We don't have time for pleasantries."

"Jeez, sorry. What's up?"

"Rule Number Six in the *Limbo Central Club Manual*."

"Okay . . . and that says?"

"That if students have scheduling conflicts with different clubs they should bring these issues up with the administration office and the teachers will be more than happy to move things around to accommodate them."

"Who has a scheduling conflict? Do you? What is it?"

"The cheerleaders."

"Oh, that's not a scheduling thing. It's a Georgia Rule. Remember? Georgia and Coach Trellis decided that the cheerleaders need to be available and healthy for all of the games, so they can't participate in other sports-related clubs."

Oliver just stands here staring at me like I'm trying to convince him chocolate is naturally fat-free.

"What? That's what Georgia said at tryouts—I heard her myself."

"And you think that's legit?"

"I think she had to have Coach okay it, otherwise she wouldn't have been allowed to announce it at tryouts."

"Well, I think it's worth pushing—out the window! There are a lot of good dancers on the squad, and if anyone can get this ridiculous rule revoked, it's Ms. Tilly. Your advisor is the *principal*, hello?!"

"Hello to you, too!" sings a voice in my left ear. "What's up?"

"Oh, hey, Mia!" I say. "This is Oliver, Oliver this is Mia."

"Do you dance?" he asks, matter-of-factly.

"Very poorly and only when provoked."

Mia and I share a laugh, but Oliver won't be led off course.

"I'm Oliver. It's nice to meet you. But you're of no use to us right now."

"Well, I'm very sorry to hear that. What's the problem? Limbos emergency?"

"We need to figure out a way to get the girls on the Cheerleading squad to be allowed on the Limbos," Oliver says.

"Oh, right, the new rule . . ." Mia says. "Well, perhaps it would interest you to know that this one-sport-only rule only seems to apply to the girls on the Cheerleading squad and no other sports teams. For instance, the boys can be on as many sports teams as they like."

"Are you serious?" Oliver gasps.

"That's . . . well, that's sexist!" I say, outraged.

"Yes, yes it is," Mia replies.

"Unacceptable!" Oliver says. "You are a genius!" he adds to Mia.

Just then the first bell rings. Mia and I are heading in one direction, while Oliver is going in another.

"I have to go to class now, but we'll discuss the plan at lunch!" he yells.

"Yes, Captain!" I say, fake saluting him as he heads off. Then I turn to Mia. "Okay, I know I've only known that kid for, like, a day and a half, but he's quickly becoming one of my absolute favorite people."

"Ha-ha, nice! So, how's the preparation for the show on Saturday night coming? Did you choose your photos yet?"

"Ugh, no! I took some nice shots on Sunday, but I still need to develop them and I might need to take some more if they're no good. Plus, I need to come up with a theme for my exhibit. I don't want to just put out a bunch of random photos; I want them to tie together somehow."

"Well, you have until Saturday afternoon to figure it out, right?"

"Yeah, I guess. So, are you and Trey coming to the show, then?"

"Of course! We wouldn't miss it."

"Thanks—that means a lot. I mean, I know you got invited to Georgia's party first and—"

"Please be quiet, like, now," she says, jokingly, as we sit down in our seats.

"Okay, fine."

"So . . . how are things with you and Cecily? Seems like you made up?"

"Yeah, we did. And I wanted to tell you that the talk we had really helped me. So thank you."

"Anytime, girl. I had a feeling she was coming around."

"Oh, yeah, how come?"

"Well, she kind of asked to crash in my room on Saturday night—"

"So *that's* where she was!"

"She was upset, you know. She didn't know where to go and she wasn't ready to talk to you yet. But she and I had a really good talk, so I figured things were heading in the right direction."

"You know what, Mia?"

"What?"

"You're a pretty awesome friend."

"Thanks, Luce."

"How would you and Trey like to model for me after school today? I just got an idea for a show theme, and you'd be perfect for it."

"I'm in. As long as you don't make me dance!"

"I make no promises," I joke.

The second bell rings, and we all settle down. Ms. Roslyn starts talking but I'm way too lost in my own thoughts to pay any attention, and I can't wipe this smile off my face.

I'm going to CRUSH this art show.

Literally.

THE LIMBO CENTRAL CLUB MANUAL

RULE #7:

Every club should have an appointed vice president or second-in-command, as well as a secretary. The members of the club should vote democratically on these positions.

Chapter Ten
The Georgia Rule

After school, Mia, Trey, and I head to a parking lot down one of the side streets off Death Row to take some pictures. I'm not a fan of the too-posed pic, so I instruct them to lie on the ground and talk to each other—to act like I'm not here—while I shoot a bunch of photos from different angles.

There's this one moment when Trey is on his stomach telling Mia something, and she's still lying on her back, literally dying of laughter.

Okay, not literally dying.

Literally, dead. And laughing.

"She walked straight into the glass door, like, for real," he says in between hysterics, "and then spun around all dizzy and stepped on the bottom of one of those big push brooms and it, like, catapulted up and smacked her in the face. I laughed so hard I think I tore a muscle."

"She did not!" Mia scream-laughs.

"It was seriously the best thing I've ever seen in my life, hands down," he says.

I scroll back through the photos I took, and think I see the winner. Since Mia is still cracking up, I use this opportunity to find out what Trey can tell me about my new totally-out-of-my-league potential crush.

"Trey, how well do you know Miles?"

"Pretty well, I guess. Why?"

"I don't know, just wondering what he's like. Is he nice? Who does he hang out with?"

"He's a cool guy. Really talented. Really into his music. He's always talking about touring with the band and stuff when he gets out of school. He and his brother, Oliver, used to go to North Limbo Junior High before they transferred here, so I think he still has a lot of friends there who he hangs out with."

"And girls?" Mia prods, helping me out.

"Uhm, I think he had a girlfriend from North Limbo, but I don't know if they're still together or what. He usually goes for the, ahem, older ladies," he says, smirking.

"Perfect," I say. "Even more proof."

"More proof of what?" Trey says.

"More proof that I should stop wasting my precious energy on boys and focus it on my show. I think I have what I need from you guys, though. Thank you for being excellent models!"

Later that night, I send a Tabulator message to the Limbos club members announcing that at Friday's meeting we'll be voting on the VP and secretary positions, and whoever would like to run should let me know by tomorrow and prepare a mini speech to deliver on Friday before the vote.

Within three seconds, I get a Holomail back from Oliver. Love this kid!

This 3-D image of Oliver leaps out of the Tabulator and screams, "I'm running for VP!!!! But I'm sure you guessed that already! OMG, we are going to make a totally insane team. First order of business? Getting that dumb Georgia Rule revoked. Let's hit Ms. Tilly's office tomorrow during lunch, deal?! Sweet dreams, Prez."

I smile wide and chuckle to myself.

Just then, Cecily comes out of the bathroom. "What's so funny?" she asks eagerly.

"Oliver."

"What'd he say?"

"He just sent a Holomail about wanting to run for VP of the Limbos."

"And? What was so funny?"

"Oh, I don't know. He wants to revoke the 'Georgia Rule,' and the way he said it made me laugh," I tell her.

"So . . . you think Oliver is going to be your VP, then?"

"We'll see who else runs, but I think he's a pretty strong candidate. What about on the squad? Who's Georgia's number two?"

"Some third year named Kelly. I don't know her all that well."

"Oh. So that's not something you can run for then?"

"Nah, new squad members aren't allowed to run."

"Another Georgia Rule?"

"The girl can't help herself," Cecily replies, half smirking.

I smirk back and lift my right eyebrow in defiance. "Perhaps someone will have to do it for her then."

On Thursday, right after the fourth-period bell rings, Oliver meets me in the administration office.

"Do we need to go over what you're going to say one more time?" he asks me, anxiously.

"Nope, I'm good! I got this!" I say, enthusiastically.

"Well, don't go wasting your energy on me," he says, swatting at me with his hand like I'm a fly.

"You need to relax," I tell him, grabbing his shoulders and shaking him from side to side.

"Why does everyone always tell me that?"

Just then, the secretary informs us that Ms. Tilly is ready.

"Well, hello there, Limbo dancers," she says. "What can I do for you?"

Before I can utter a breath, let alone an actual word, Oliver begins to speak emphatically, and rather loudly.

"Georgia Sinclaire has imposed a rule on her Cheerleading squad that is completely and totally sexist and cannot be tolerated! It's impacting the Limbos, and it's offensive to all of us!" he commands.

"Oh boy, this sounds very serious. What is this rule?"

I give Oliver a look that says, "I got this one."

I explain the sexist rule and how it only targets the cheerleaders, and even though I swore I would keep my cool (unlike Oliver!), I get all worked up and finish my perfect speech with a lame and whiny, "It's just . . . well . . . it's completely uncool!"

"Oh dear," Ms. Tilly says. "You're very right. It is completely *uncool*. I had no idea when Coach Trellis ran this by me that it would only apply to the cheerleaders. I thought it would apply to everyone on every team."

"Nope," Oliver says. "And there are a lot of cheerleaders who wanted to sign up for the Limbos, but now they aren't allowed to. It's extremely unfair."

"I'll discuss this with Coach Trellis at once," she says. "We simply cannot have rules that apply to one team and not the others, or worse, to girls and not to boys. Our rules at Limbo must be kept equal at all times. And thank you for bringing this to my attention."

"You're very welcome," I reply, resisting my urge to jump up and down screaming, "Take that, Black Mop Head!"

"So, in other Limbos news, are you both excited about our vote tomorrow?" she asks.

"I'm running for VP!" Oliver says, beaming.

"And judging by the way you handled this situation, young man, you'll make a fine VP."

"Thank you, Principal Tilly," Oliver replies.

We leave her office triumphant and head to the cafeteria to grab some lunch before fifth period. Oliver joins us at our table, and I use this as an opportunity to take some more candid shots of people for my show. (Colin basically just let me keep his camera for the week.)

Oliver starts to tell Cecily about our meeting with Ms. Tilly, and how he's so sure she's going to revoke the Georgia Rule . . . and that's when it happens—and I'm snapping pictures the whole time.

"So do you really think she's going to throw out the rule?" Cecily asks him.

"Yes, I really do. She was, like, appalled that it applied only to you ladies. I actually think she looked embarrassed—and rightfully so. I mean, that rule sets back the women's movement by, like, decades."

Click.

"Right . . ." Cecily says, looking completely deflated. "Why didn't I think of that? I mean, I just accepted it, no questions asked."

"She's got you brainwashed, that's why!" Oliver chimes. "I mean, why should girls have to sacrifice their passions just so the boys can have their cheerleaders at games on Friday nights?" Oliver went on. "It's totally archaic."

"You're right!" Cecily says, with more pep and fire now. "Who is she to tell me that I can't be on the Limbos because the boys' needs come first?! You know what? I'm doing the Limbos. Forget this rule, and forget Georgia!"

Georgia, who just happens to be sitting on the other end of our table, doesn't seem to hear Cecily's outburst.

"Well, I'm pretty sure we've already gotten the rule outlawed," Oliver reminds her.

"Oh, right. Well, I'm gonna take it further, then!" Cecily says.

Oliver and I exchange glances. Is she having some kind of psychotic episode or something?

"I'm not just going to be on the Limbos—I'm gonna be your VP, Lou."

Click.

Uh-oh.

"That's if you'll be okay with that," she goes on. "I mean, I know you originally wanted me to be a co-captain, and VP isn't the same thing exactly, but it's just as good, I think. Don't you?"

I did not see this coming.

This is what I've been wanting since this whole thing started—for Cecily to want to be a part of the Limbos and for the two of us to dance together again, and run this club together. And yet, now that Oliver is involved and so excited about it all, I feel torn. He Holomailed me about running for

VP the *second* he got my message. He didn't hesitate AT ALL. I don't think it would be fair to give it to Cecily now, after everything that's happened. I mean, don't get me wrong, it's great that she suddenly wants to stand up to Georgia. But . . . it's too late for things to go back to exactly the way they were. Things are different now. Oliver is in the picture, and I owe him something.

"The thing is, Cece," I say, lowering the camera from my face. "We have to have open elections for the VP and secretary spots now. You know that Oliver is already running for VP. You can run, too, if you want. But, we have to let the Limbos vote now that we're already a formed club."

"Oh, right, of course," she says, quietly, looking down. "That makes sense. You'd make a great VP, Oliver."

I can tell she feels embarrassed. I want to tell her not to, but it's awkward with Oliver sitting here, so I don't say anything.

Just then, as if on cue, Coach Trellis comes up to our table—to the other side, where Georgia and Colin are sitting with Jonah and some other football players and cheerleaders. She whispers something in Georgia's ear, and within three seconds Georgia is staring me down with the biggest, mean-est, most dramatic death stare anyone has ever seen.

Mission accomplished.

(Our mission, not hers. *I'm* already dead, so she CAN'T take credit for that!)

"Guess Coach delivered the bad news," Oliver says with a huge smile on his face, lifting up his hand to high-five me.

I return the high five in celebration.

And snap a picture of the moment for posterity.

Click.

By Friday evening, Cecily, Oliver, and I are completely and totally pooped.

On Thursday afternoon, Cecily had cheerleading practice and Georgia broke the news to the squad: Her rule is off and they are free to join whatever clubs they want without being penalized, as long as they "remain *dedicated*" to the squad.

While Cecily was at practice, I was in the dark room developing some of the photos I've taken this week and narrowing down which ones I'm going to display at the exhibit. And Oliver was frantically writing his VP election speech and then rehearsing it over and over and over and over and over again.

And then over again, again.

It's a wonder we made it through Limbos practice and open elections at all!

But we did.

And now we're all lying on the sand at the beach and the sun is setting and nothing could be more perfect than this.

"So, VP, how are we going to get your brother together with Lou?" Cecily asks Oliver.

"Cece!" I screech. "I'm off boys, remember? I'm focusing on my art now."

"Focus, schmocus," Cecily says.

"The secretary makes a valid point," Oliver says. "Focus, schmocus, indeed!"

"Oh, would you two knock it off?" I cry out, laughing. "Can we just please get through this weekend—Georgia's stupid ghostday party and my show—without any more drama for one week?"

Cecily scrunches up her face and turns to me. "Would now be a bad time to tell you that because you had her rule revoked, Georgia told us all at practice yesterday that she is requiring the whole squad to show up to The Cove at six tomorrow to help her set up for her party?"

"Ahhhhhhhhhhhhhhhhhhhhhhhhh!" I scream as loud and as long as my breath can stand it.

"I'll take that as a yes," she whispers. "I'm sorry."

"And if you don't go?"

"I think she'll try to have me thrown off the squad, you know, for not being *dedicated* or showing team spirit or something."

"Right."

"Look, I'll just go at six and leave as soon as we're done setting up."

"Sure. Whatever," I say. I can't get mad at her, but I can't pretend it doesn't bother me, either.

The Georgia Whack-a-Mole is here to stay. Every time I slam her face down, she's just gonna pop back up screaming, "Georgia Lives 4Ever!"

Georgia Lives 4Evil is more like it.

"Okay, let's get back on topic, people! Focus, please," Oliver says. "Regarding the Miles situation, a little birdie told me you might want to wear something red to your big show tomorrow night."

"What does *that* mean?" I ask, nervously, as the sun becomes completely enveloped by the ocean off in the distance.

He looks at me slyly. "*You* know what it means, Prez."

Do red cheeks count?

If so, check!

THE
LIMBO CENTRAL
CLUB MANUAL

RULE #8:

Although these clubs are school-sanctioned activities, there are requirements that are bound to take place outside of school grounds. Your elected club presidents have earned the right to decide which of those activities are deemed necessary, and you should have faith in their judgment. Some clubs have more of these requirements than others, so take that into consideration when choosing the club that is right for you.

Chapter Eleven
Red Is a Color

Grrr.

I can't decide what to wear.

It's three thirty P.M. on Saturday afternoon, and I hate what I have on. I tried on four different outfits before this one, and I hated all of those, too. I keep hearing Oliver's voice in my head telling me to wear red and I'm two seconds away from screaming, "Shut it, Oliver!" at the top of my lungs.

Except *that* would be pointless, because Oliver isn't actually here. He's in my brain. Here's the thing: Does wearing red make me seem totally pathetic, like I'll do anything to make a boy like me? Because, at this point, I'm not even sure that I like Miles . . . Or, does it mean I can be open-minded and take advice from my friends who clearly just want what's best for me? Will it be completely and totally obvious to Miles that I'm only wearing red because Oliver told me that he likes it? Or can red just, like, be a color that people wear sometimes, and I just happen to be wearing it tonight?

"*What* is the problem this time?" Cecily finally speaks, after watching me stare at myself in the mirror in silence for the last ten minutes.

"I don't like it," I grumble.

"What's not to like? You look awesome! Your outfit is perfect! It's cool and kind of rock star–like without being over the top. It says, 'I'm a hip photographer, and I hang out with hip, artsy types, and I'm totally into hip keyboard players who are in bands,'" she finishes, crossing her arms, quite pleased with herself.

"Does it have to say *hip* so much?!" I cry out. "That's, like, three *hips*! That's *way* too many."

"I'm just trying to be down with the artsy lingo," she says, kidding around. "I'm not into the scene like you are . . ."

"You need to stop talking immediately."

"Okay, fine, that's not what it says. It says, 'I'm a little dressy but not too dressy, I'm artistic but still down to earth, and I like the color red.'"

"That's it, I'm changing my jeans. No one wears red jeans, anyway!"

"Yes, they do! Just stop, please. You look great. You're just freaking out."

"I don't want it to say, 'I like the color red.' That's way too obvious."

"Okay, what would you like it to say instead, Lou?" she asks, exasperated.

"I want it to say, 'Red . . . is a color.' The end."

"You? Are cuckoo-pants right now."

"So you're saying you think I should change the pants?"

"Get out of here. Now."

It's three forty-five, and I have to be at the museum by four. I grab my bag with my five framed photos and head for the door.

"Okay, so I'll be there as close to seven as possible," Cecily says. "Don't be nervous."

"Impossible."

"Don't change your outfit."

"I'll try."

"Don't make anything explode."

"Fat chance."

"And, finally, break a leg!"

"Thanks."

I arrive at the museum at four on the nose, and it's bustling with young ghosts of all ages and artwork of all mediums. It's not just kids from school—in fact, I don't recognize most of the people here. Which is kind of cool, when you think about it. I mean, this exhibit is for students from all over Limbo Central, and that includes the high schools, too!

I go over to the sign-in area, and one of the organizers shows me to my little corner where I can hang my photos.

"We have a nameplate for you waiting to be printed and mounted," the girl says, "but we need the title of your exhibit. Go over to the desk by the back wall—do you see it?" I nod. "Tell them who you are and what your exhibit is called and they'll get it ready for you."

"Great, thanks!"

I didn't realize how professional this would all be, and I suddenly start to get nervous.

It takes me almost forty minutes to align my photos and hang them the way I want them, then I wait in line by the back table for ten minutes for my nameplate, and by the time I'm finished setting up, the show is basically starting. I secure the nameplate in place, and when I step back and take in the whole visual, I'm really pleased.

Each photo fits in its own perfect way. There's the sweet shot of Mia and Trey on the paved parking lot ground, laughing. Trey has his hands on the sides of her head. Her knees are bent in and she's clutching her stomach in laughter. *Crushed Together.* There's the close-up of Georgia's shocked expression right after Cecily first mentioned coming to my show before her ghostday party. *Crushed Up.* The photo of Oliver and me high-fiving after we got the Georgia Rule revoked. *Crushed It.* There's the image of Cecily at lunch the other day realizing that she let Georgia brainwash her into doing something she didn't believe in. *Crushed Into.* And, of course, there's the original photo of Miles from the show, playing the keyboards and singing during the gig. *Crushed and . . .*

"What does the *and* stand for?" a voice from behind me asks.

I turn around and Miles and Oliver are standing there. Oliver has a knowing smirk on his face. I turn my attention toward Miles, who asked the question.

"Hey! Uhm, it means there's more to the story."

"Like?"

"Like, I'm not sure yet," I say, smiling nervously.

"That's fair," he replies.

"Love the outfit!" Oliver says, coming in for a hug. "This color is fab on you."

"What, this?" I stutter, anxious. "It's just . . . red. Red is a color."

Oliver looks at me like my brain has just been surgically removed. "Yeah, I know it's a color. Are you okay? Do you need me to get you something, like a chair . . . or a doctor?"

"Oh, no, no. No," I reply, sounding even creepier than before.

What. Is. My. Problem?!

"Hey, thanks for coming!" I say, trying to change the tone of the conversation.

"Well, I *am* part of your exhibit," Miles says, "so I had to support my rise to stardom."

"Ah, yes, of course."

"Oh—there's Sasha, Allie, and Lara from the Limbos!" Oliver calls out, running toward them. "You're going the wrong way! She's over here, on the other side!"

"I *love* your brother," I tell Miles, when Oliver is gone. "I mean, seriously, he's the coolest. He's, like, not afraid of anyone or anything. That's really rare."

"Yeah, he's a pretty cool dude," Miles says. "And a seriously nosy dude. I mean, try having any secrets with that kid in the house."

"Ha-ha, yeah, I can imagine."

"It's like he's the older brother, always telling me what's best for me. Always thinking he knows what I want and sticking his nose in everything. I mean, he even tries to choose my girlfriends, telling girls private stuff about me, like what my favorite color is so they can color coordinate their outfits and things like that."

My stomach drops to the floor, and I feel my face go white.

At least I hope it goes white, because if it's turning red? I'm a goner.

"Blue," he says, in conclusion, "in case you were wondering."

"Blue's a good color," I reply, noticing in that moment that he is, in fact, wearing a blue T-shirt.

Kill me now.

"I'm a gray girl, myself," I finally say, because I can't stand the silence anymore.

"Really? I had you for a red girl," he says. Then he winks at me and walks away.

I can't tell if he's being cute or if he's mocking me. I want to crawl into a hole. Why did I listen to Oliver and Cecily? I should have followed my gut and changed my outfit. I have no idea what actually transpired between Miles and me, but it's either one of two things:

1. He knows I wore red because Oliver told me to and was just mocking me with the whole blue comment.
   or
2. His favorite color is actually blue and he was telling me all that stuff to prove to me that Oliver doesn't really know anything about who he does and does not like.

Either way? I'm going to re-die of total mortification any second now. Luckily, with everyone dispersed, I have a little while to myself to regain my composure. I decide to do a lap around the museum to check out the other students' work. After about a half hour, I end up back at my corner just as

Oliver is ushering the three Limbos members into my section. It's around eight o'clock, and there's no sign of Cecily.

Georgia Lives 4Evil.

"They totally got lost!" Oliver says, as I greet the newcomers.

While they look at my photos, I pull Oliver aside. "What is wrong with you?" I reprimand him.

"Uhm, excuse me? *What* is wrong with *you*?" he shoots back.

"Miles totally humiliated me earlier. Told me that you're always telling girls he likes them and then forcing them to wear his favorite color!"

"He told you it was blue, didn't he?"

"YES! Wait, how do you know that?"

"Duh, he's just messing with you. He wanted to see your face——if you got all flustered and embarrassed and turned ten shades of white, that means you wore red for him and you like him, too."

"But he said you always think you know what's best for him . . . and that . . ."

"Yeah, and? I do. And he knows it."

"But he said it like it wasn't true."

"You need to relax and trust me."

"Hey, guys!" another voice from the crowd calls out. It's Mia. "Luce, this is awesome! I love your corner. It's very professional."

She and Trey pull themselves into our little circle of conversation.

"What'd we miss? Lucy, you look like someone just died."

"Someone did," I confirm.

"Oh no, who?" she says, concerned. "Someone you know?"

"Yes!" I cry out. "ME!"

"Oh, I get it," Mia says, and then turns to Oliver. "She's freaking out about something."

"What else is new!" he says, throwing up his hands.

"We've only known each other, like, three days!" I say to Oliver. "You can't possibly know how often I freak out yet."

"Prove me wrong," he replies, and then says this: "Mia, what do you think about Lucy's outfit? Don't you just love the color?"

"Actually, I do!" she answers, full of enthusiasm. "It's very rock star. And you are killing it in red."

I pout as I look at the two of them, trying not to burst into tears.

Or make someone else burst into flames.

"Red is a color," I whine.

Oliver puts his hand on my back. "It sure is, sweetie."

"Hey look, there's the photo of us," Trey says, spotting it hanging on the wall. "Wow, we look *good*."

"You're such a dork," Mia says, laughing.

I can't help but smirk. Trey always knows how to lighten the mood.

By now, it's almost eight thirty and I'm starting to get peeved, when I hear a very loud "Congratulations!"

Cecily is standing in front of my corner with almost all of Georgia's cheerleading squad. Okay, not all of them—but a lot of them.

"I'm so, so, so sorry we're late," she says, giving me a big hug. "Georgia was on another level tonight. Every time we wanted to leave she kept threatening to throw us off the squad until finally I was like, 'Do what you want, I don't care! I refuse to be held hostage. This is insane!' and most of the squad felt the same way. It's one thing to be bossed around at practice, but the weekend is our time. It's not like we were doing anything even remotely related to cheerleading! Anyway, a bunch of them decided to come here with us, and there's no way she's kicking all of us off the squad."

"Wow, sounds intense," I remark.

I look at my little area and I see Chloe, her friend Briana, Marcus, and, like, four other girls on the squad who I haven't met yet.

"Your photos are so cool," Chloe tells me. "You should totally be a professional photographer!"

"Thanks, Chloe. It was really nice of you to come."

"Well, we definitely wanted to see your show, but we also wanted to show support for our Limbos president," she replies, with a smile. "Briana and I are back on board now that that stupid rule has been dropped."

"That's amazing! The Limbos would love to have you."

Marcus also brought along the rest of their Figure of Speech band members, so all in all, there are a lot of people here for me.

The only person who isn't here? Colin.

Not that I'm surprised or anything. But it doesn't have to be surprising to be a giant bummer, does it?

At nine o'clock, the award ceremony takes place. I don't win the first-place prize of my own gallery show—that goes to Noah Jennings for his incredible, three-dimensional light installation. But I do get an honorable mention award.

Imagine that. Me? Honorable.

Then, as if out of thin air, Colin appears before me.

"I'm sorry you didn't win," he says. "You would have been my pick."

"Thanks," I reply, pleasantly surprised. "What are you doing here? How did you manage to break free?"

I'm pretty sure if Georgia knew he was here right now, she'd split a rib screaming.

"It was time to go," he says.

"The party's over already?" I ask, confused. "Seems early."

"No, I mean it was time . . . for me, to go. Like, for good. Me and Georgia? We're just no good together. I keep thinking she'll learn from her mistakes, but . . ." He trails off.

"Yeah, people are funny that way," I reply, raising my eyebrow and smiling, knowingly.

I wonder if he realizes I'm thinking about him and how he hasn't learned from his mistakes any more than Georgia has learned from hers. I hope so, but I know it's doubtful.

He smiles at me, and there's that adorable dimple, all shiny and happy.

Stupid dimple.

"Well, I'll leave you to it," he says, backing away. "You've got so many adoring fans, I don't want to monopolize your time. Congratulations, Lucy."

Cecily bounces over to me right after Colin takes his leave. I want to fill her in on what just happened, but there are too many people here for us to talk privately.

"Lou, this is amazing! I'm so proud of you!" she squeals happily.

"Thanks, Cece. You know what? I'm kind of proud of me, too."

"You should be!" She puts her arm around me, and we survey the room. "Hey, look, there's Miles!"

I look in the direction she's facing, but I can't spot him in the crowd. "Where? I don't see him?"

"Right over there," she says, pointing at some guy a ways away. "The tall guy in the red T-shirt."

"He's wearing a blue shirt, not a red one," I reply, only I can't deny that it does look distinctly like Miles from behind.

And then red-shirt guy turns around and it *is* Miles. He starts walking toward me.

"Incoming!" Cecily trills. She heads off to find Marcus as Miles reappears by my side.

"You kind of threw me there, for a minute," I tell him. "What happened to blue?"

"Oliver was right," he says, smiling. "I really do like red better."

I see Oliver, Mia, and Cecily across the room and a huge rush of happiness runs through me.

And then I spot Colin. Still here.

What's that saying about how the three areas of your life can never be drama-free all at the same time?

Friends? Peas in a pod. Check!

School? Studies are solid, Limbos are golden. Check!

Boys? *Crushed and Confused.*

Just another day in the afterlife of your average ghost, I suppose. And this ghost? Is off to celebrate her honorable mention with the most honorable friends anyone could ask for in a slightly revised outfit that says, "I'm really lucky. I crushed this show. And this afterlife is gonna be KILLER."

Did you see where the Afterlife drama all started?
Don't miss

HAPPILY EVER
AFTERLIFE

Ghostcoming!

Turn the page for a sneak peek!

We walk back out into the main office and to my relief, the mean girl and her sidekick are nowhere to be seen. I'm so focused on making sure she isn't around, that I completely overlook the ghost who is.

"Lucy Chadwick, this is Colin Reed," Ms. Keaner says, introducing Mr. Perfect Ghost Boy from earlier. "Here is your schedule, and these are your books," she continues, handing them to Colin. "He'll be carrying your things for you until you are strong enough to carry them yourself."

"Hey, Lucy," Colin says, smiling.

I extend my hand to shake hello, and he slowly extends his, too, cautiously, like he's confused about my plan.

This should faze me, but it doesn't.

I reach over, and because I am so intent on producing a nice, strong handshake to show how awesomely confident I am, the force of my swing-and-miss throws me shoulder first into Colin's chest as if I am tackling him at the twenty-yard line.

Except that I don't *actually* tackle him because I CAN'T DO THAT EITHER! So I pass right through his chest and *BOOM*! I wind up floating flat on my face an inch away from the floor. I literally just threw myself on the ground for no apparent reason.

Mortified.

"I'm sorry," I mutter, wishing I had remembered that I can't perform most of the things I learned to do by the age of six. "That was so stupid of me. Oh, god, I went right through your body, didn't I? Talk about an invasion of privacy . . . I'm sorry, I'm so sorry."

If my face weren't completely see-through, it would be bright red right about now.

"Don't worry about it," he replies, laughing. "It happens to all of us when we first get here. It took me almost two months to learn how to change my clothes—don't be so hard on yourself. Come on, let's go find your first class."

Okay . . . so, things *could* be worse. Having Colin carry my things, show me around school, and teach me the ropes one-on-one doesn't sound half-bad, right? Then again, it's only Day 1 of my new life (I mean, *afterlife*), so I could still be wrong.

Dead wrong.

Orli Zuravicky is a writer, an editor, and an amateur interior designer, which basically means she likes to paint stuff in her apartment. She has been in children's publishing for fifteen years and has written over sixty-five books for children. She hopes to write sixty-five more. She lives her happily ever after (life) in Brooklyn, New York.